W	O	R	L	D	M	U	S	E	S
O									E
R									S
L			R	H	Y	S			U
D									M
M									D
U			H	U	G	H	E	S	L
S									R
E									O
S	E	S	U	M	D	L	R	O	W

"The world is a ball and our minds are a room and our lives are an endless dance in the ballrooms of forsaken palaces on those smaller worlds called our hearts, where seismic activity is almost constant, for the geology of our emotions is still young. The volcanic upthrusts of our yearnings make mountains out of our hopes and inspiration shakes the earth and collapses it beneath us and we wish for our fears to turn out to be groundless too. And sometimes indeed they are."

How does one dedicate a book that itself is already an extended dedication? I dedicate this book to Diversity and Inspiration rather than to an individual, for there is no reason why a book can't be dedicated to concepts or ideals.

World Muses

Rhys Hughes

Gloomy Seahorse Press

ISBN-13: 978-1979367905

ISBN-10: 1979367906

Gloomy Seahorse Press
http://gloomyseahorsepress.blogspot.com

The Muses:

Ayu
Zelina
Amber
Selam
Lubna
Marie
Shubha
Isabel
Dolly
Mengjie
Elodie
Itxaso
Vanessa
Zsuzsanna
Peppiina
Insyirah
Jimena
Flutura
Cyrine
Amivi
Charlotte
Arabella
Oksana/Ksenya
Tabarak
Eilah
Aleksandra
Simone
Eleftheria
Lisandra

Thérèse
Olivia
Anahita
Misaki
Marguerite
Nadine
Giuliana
Lowri
Claudetta
Océane
Jessica
Danique
Bhagya
Kwame
Nadja
Dusica
Lucy
Viviana
Silvia
Ji-su
Yasmine
Buivasa
Raveena
Franziska
Jennifer
Brankica
Mona
Dagmara
Saturnina

Esther
Söökhlö
Ophelia
Sreyneang
Stella
Amira
Catarina
Emily
Princessa
Jane
Sandy
Joramae
Yousra
Hilola
Tameris
Georgina
Siranush (1)
Parisa
Siranush (2)
Chlöe
Ernestina
Anonymia
Monica
Alice
Rebekah
Samantha
Verniana
Envoi
& You

Many thanks to the magnificent **Kwame Devonish**, who gave me permission to use her image on the cover of this book.

"Out of the red and silver and the long cry of alarm to the poet who survives in all human beings, as the child survives in him; to this poet she threw an unexpected ladder in the middle of the city and ordained, 'Climb!"

— Anaïs Nin

"Today I'm out wandering, turning my skull into a cup for others to drink wine from. In this town somewhere there sits a calm, intelligent man, who doesn't know what he's about to do!"

— Mevlana Jelaluddin Rumi

Ayu

AYU WAS FROM INDONESIA and was already part of the dance class when I joined. I had never met anyone from her country before. She was nice to dance with because she had an unusual style that was graceful and elegant and that no one else could copy. It was unique to her. The rest of us just held onto each other and when we let go, in order to perform a spin, we didn't do anything special with our hands.

She told me that she knew the traditional dances of her culture and that some of their moves, especially the positioning of the hands and the expressions of her face, could be used even in the kind of fast dancing we were doing in that class. It was an intriguing fusion and it worked. I fell in love with her, of course, but it was a hopeless case. She went back to her country and I wasn't able to follow her.

I then became obsessed with Indonesian things because they helped me feel closer to her, but the connection they created was an illusion. No amount of gamelan music could return her smile to me. I knew I had to forget her to protect my heart and I decided to go to the opposite extreme but I didn't know what the reverse of Indonesia was. I mused a long time about komodo dragons and their opposites.

The opposite of a dragon is a damsel, but a komodo dragon isn't a real dragon, it's a large lizard that lives on one of the thousands of islands of Indonesia. Therefore its opposite isn't a real damsel, but just a big person who doesn't need to be rescued. The largest person at the dance class was a man and it occurred to me that if I danced with him, then I would cancel out Ayu, not that I wanted to cancel her out.

But it was for the best. These things are always for the best. When we become obsessive fools, we waste our lives. So I invited the biggest man to dance and he was surprised at first but agreed. We both tried to lead the dance at the same time, for that was the only way we knew. We pulled in opposite directions and although he was the largest man in the class, I am the second largest. It was a difficult struggle.

Somehow we ended up getting all entangled with our arms twisted in unbreakable knots, and to be honest the doctors thought it would be better not to even attempt to separate us. Ayu is a Hindu from Bali and in her faith there are gods with more than two arms. I have four arms now, and even though two aren't strictly mine, I still feel like one of the deities she pays her devotions to, in some distant temple.

Zelina

I CALL HER MY sunlight girl because when she appears the darkness of long nights and the gloom of narrow rooms seems to vanish. This is a paradox because she is dark all over, her skin, eyes and hair are an intense ebony colour, and yet the vibrancy of her presence is a tangible glow that can be seen as well as felt.

Other people are lost in shadows, they merge with the umbrae and melt their shapes and they might as well be broken umbrellas huddling in a lonely corner out of the rain. But Zelina casts light when she walks, her shadow a negative of mine and yours, and she can always see where she is going. We follow her like lost children. She is lithe, faster, more graceful than we are, and soon we are left behind, even when mounted on bicycles. We lose our balance in the murk, we collide and tumble, calling, "Zelina, come back!" But she never does, and why should she?

I call her my sunlight girl but she is not mine. She is nobody's; she is only herself. In winter before the dawn, when the wind rises and the cold is so deep inside my bones that I feel they will snap like icicles and I will become a jellyfish man, a loose sack of splinters, unable to ride or stand or maintain any coherent shape, I seek her out. I never find her but I sometimes come across her footprints, perfectly formed and beautiful, not only in the sand but also on the flagstones of the public squares, and full of crackling fire. I crouch over them, rub my hands together.

Are all the women in your country like you, Zelina? I am just a simple dreamer and I dream about you, but without greed or anger, because I try to appreciate you for what you are, not for what I want from you. And yet I warm myself on the flames of your footprints and use you in this way. I even take out a saucepan to brew coffee there and then, or hot chocolate, and close my eyes as I sip and see behind my eyelids not deeper darkness but lights that leap like solar flares, like you.

Amber

BUTTERFLIES HAVE BEEN FOUND preserved in amber, but your name is Amber and you are the butterfly, so I guess the amber must be inside you. Maybe your heart is a fist of fossilised tree sap, but no, that image isn't romantic enough and gives a misleading impression of who you are. I hardly know you but I am sure your heart is softer than my clumsy metaphor. Not that amber is hard or rough or cold, far from it.

You told me you were from the Virgin Islands and I replied that I was from the Isle of Man, just a joke, of course, but one that demonstrates my iron will. I can resist the urge to be charming and sweet, to melt before an image of beauty and vibrancy. You laughed tolerantly. But the fact is that islands never break free and float towards each other. Ships collide but an island never ventures beyond its own surf.

You are a person I admire from a distance and I lack sufficient reason to cover you with the sentimental sediment of sonorous phrases and wait for it to harden over aeons of time, to try fixing you fast in poetics. What does it mean anyway to babble pretty gibberish in praise of a woman who is a dream for me at this moment, a yearning? If you do possess an amber heart, then the butterfly within is still alive.

I can almost hear it fluttering when I approach you. If amber is rubbed with cloth it briefly becomes magnetic. When the tip of a butterfly's wing constantly brushes an amber heart from inside, that magnetic field will be intense enough to draw men, this man, to you over any distance. But in the presence of magnetism, iron is weak. I am a man with an iron will. If only it were another metal, I might be safe.

Selam

WE PLAYED VOLLEYBALL ON the beach and you hit the ball up with such force that it never came down. I asked if you played volleyball that way back in Ethiopia and you nodded, but I only saw your nod from a corner of an eye because I was still looking at the sky.

Do eyes have corners, despite the fact they are round? Yes, they must do, otherwise no one would have invented the saying and had it accepted. When I said it, you knew what I meant. I saw you nod from the corner of an eye, Selam, your curly headed nod.

The sky too must have corners if an eye can, even though it's a dome, and the ball clearly was stuck in one of those corners. Your black hair can tumble forever over your shoulders but the ball is never tumbling again. It has taken up residence in the heavens.

You sat on the sand and brewed coffee on the embers of the fire and it would have been blissful to join you, to accept your invitation and sip a sweet blackness with my lips while drinking a sweeter blackness with my gaze, but I was worried about that ball.

What if it came down after all, and landed on an innocent bystander? I kept watching it without moving from my own footprints, a shrinking dot in the cloudless blue. The hours passed and the sun went down and it was bedtime for the daylight things up there.

But I didn't yet know if the ball was an artefact of light or darkness, if it was cousin to the sun or the moon. You stood and took my hand to lead me away from my vigil. The ball has gone, it is just something that occurs now and again, you explained. I nodded.

In your presence, Selam, I often lose my head. I wonder if one day the feeling will manifest itself as an actuality and it will rise off my shoulders and enter that celestial region where all the lost balls are waiting. I really ought to take care to nod less vigorously.

Lubna

I MET LUBNA THE day after I bought myself a pair of strong stout shoes. I was tired of my shoes falling apart after a few months, so I spent extra money to purchase a pair that were guaranteed to last for years. Then Lubna came into my life. The two events are not thematically related but without those special shoes and without that special woman I certainly wouldn't be where I am today.

Lubna is a Sufi and she told me about her faith and I listened with interest and during our friendship my interest grew and kept growing. I did research on my own and I eventually decided that I too wanted to be a Sufi. I revealed this one quiet night while we were strolling under a sky scratched by shooting stars. My real education had begun and has lasted until the present instant.

In Pakistan the practice of Sufi whirling is called *Dhamaal* and is one of the forms of physically active meditation that fill a devotee with awareness of the ineffable and help move a questing soul closer to the source of all perfection. Lubna demonstrated the ceremony in a room in her house and my heart burned with eagerness to emulate her movements. When she finished it was my turn.

Yes, it literally was my turn. As she played the *naghara* faster and faster, I found myself spinning into a trance, keeping time with the drum, and a beautiful feeling of love and selflessness filled me. But something else happened too. Lubna was growing taller, she was now high above me, her eyes shut tight and her expression rapt as her hands fluttered over the drum in a mesmeric blaze.

Then I understood that it was me who was sinking. I was drilling myself into the ground. Soon my head was level with the floor and I opened my mouth to speak but I had nothing to say that could be louder than the drum. The *naghara* did all the talking and I was a listener descending deeper and deeper into the ground. Lubna became an increasingly distant figure impossible to focus on.

I knew I would keep spinning for as long as she played the drum, but when I was deep enough, so deep that the surface world was just a point of light at the end of an extremely long tunnel, how would I know whether she was still playing it or not? The sound would be far beyond the range of my hearing. But it would continue playing in my head because she had planted the rhythm there.

I saw many curious sights on my descent. At first the darkness increased until the blackness was almost total, then the walls of the tunnel began to redden and visibility returned, for I had penetrated beneath the crust of our planet and was now entering the zone where magma flows and glows. Deep down to the centre of the Earth I was headed on a spiritual voyage to the core of my soul.

14

I broke through caverns that were bubbles in this magma and there were strange forms of life there, and species no longer existent above, but everything was a smear, a blur, a ribbon of impressions, because I was spinning so fast. I burst those bubbles and they vanished like worlds dismissed by a cosmic force but I was unable to stop spinning, for the music was still playing in my mind.

Eventually I reached the centre of the world, but momentum carried me through it and beyond and I ended up emerging into daylight on the other side of the globe. That is where I finally came to rest, my legs standing vertical in the middle of a desert in a country I had never visited before. There was no more rock for the drill of my legs to bite on. The motor had stopped, the music had died.

Lubna, I am now a solitary tree in a barren territory, a very rare legtree. I hope one day you will rest in the inadequate shade of my feet and say a prayer. Had my shoes been less sturdy they would have worn out long before I journeyed right through the planet. Had I never met you, I could never have spun my way with such joy. I found myself in the process. Please come and find me too.

Marie

WHEN SHE STEPPED OFF the train onto the station platform, Marie decided to put on her jumper.

That's normal procedure when one feels cold. I do it myself and perhaps so do you. Her jumper was pink and thin, but let me explain. The interior of the train had been heated by artificial means and also by the fact it was full of passengers, but now we were at our destination there was only a weak sun shining on us, and although the platform was full of the same passengers, who had been disgorged along with us, our bare arms felt the chill of an inadequate summer.

I had her camera slung around my neck. I like carrying objects for her, anything at all, just to show my devotion without being too obvious or maudlin about it. We had travelled to visit friends on a faraway beach for a party and now we were back. Marie was returning to France soon. Time was short, but that's how time always is in these situations. I was both happy and sad, but I showed only the happiness or tried to. She was the way she always is, friendly but wistful, with a wistfulness that made me feel I had lost her already, though I was right next to her.

As she pulled the jumper over her head, the label on the inside caught on her nose and treated her nose like a hook in a cloakroom. The entire jumper remained draped over her head, covering her eyes and cheeks, leaving only her mouth exposed, which amused her to an extreme degree. She began laughing. The opportunity was too good to miss and I raised her camera and pointed it. She had taught me that French people say the word "Ouistiti" when having their photograph taken, and now I cried out for her to speak those magic syllables, but to no avail.

In order to improve the pictures I was taking, I bent down on one knee. Marie was shaking with mirth. The milling passengers stopped to stare and it turned out that the performance had the appearance of a religious ritual to them, Marie standing with uplifted arms and an acolyte kneeling before her and repeating, "Ouistiti! Ouistiti!" while she trembled and laughed, and soon others were pulling their shirts and jumpers over their heads and laughing, or crouching and chanting along with me, and this is how a religion came into being on a train station platform.

I am no longer the only one devoted to Marie. She has many followers, admirers, worshippers. But the truth is that there were always people who yearned and burned to be near her. Only the context of affection has changed, from physical to spiritual.

She has flown back to France but there is a prophecy that she will one day return. We remain her hopeful servants as we weave through the city streets, our heads covered by garments, the "Ouistiti" mantra on our chuck-ling lips, faithful aches in our foolish hearts, collecting new converts as we blindly proceed.

Shubha

I SAID I WOULD do anything for you but I never said I would do everything for you. The difference is considerable. I will hurry to you in the middle of the night if you summon me, on my bicycle because there is no other means of transport, down narrow lanes between the dark forest trees until I must cross the rivers in my path, then I will swim and emerge dripping on the opposite bank, and shivering in cold moonlight I will warm myself by running over the hills and become dry in the moonlit wind. Before the stars fade with the dawn I will reach your village and the house you share with your sister, whom I have never met.

Yes, I will do all this for you, Shubha, if you call for me, because my promises when they are broken are ugly things, like the dropped plates of unfinished dinners. One hesitates to put the pieces back together because they are stained with food and their touch is unpleasant. I prefer promises to remain whole, useful, aesthetically pleasing. For you, Shubha, I will do anything. It follows that I will hasten at great cost to my physical integrity to your side, if that is what you wish, because that is part of anything, but if you do summon me in this manner, and if I do arrive, bruised, battered and weary, it will be once and once only.

That is the essential difference between anything and everything. You ask me to perform a service and I will. That is my pledge. But if you ask me to do the same action again, I will decline. A repeat of my journey is unconscionable, beyond the terms of my vow, Shubha, and is asking too much. Having done it once, I am under no obligation to do it again. I have done anything for you, any one thing, and there is no need to duplicate the ordeal, for that would be to do everything instead. I have brought the glove you left at my house, as you requested, and here it is. But no, I will not go back for the other one, I am sorry.

Isabel

THE HOUSE WE LIVED in was in a poor part of the city and one morning we woke up and looked through the bedroom window and saw an enormous drunken fire burning in a lane at the rear of our building. Flames lurched and staggered and sometimes leaped as if trying to catch murderous hold of the branches of the rotten trees in our decaying garden. Brown smoke twisted and coiled like Isabel's thick hair.

It was not a clean fire and I said to her, "A drunkard has set alight all this rubbish and the fire is his child and maybe we can identify the culprit from its features." But her response was to cuff my whimsy and then pout with her hands on her hips. Even through the shut window we could hear the ferocious crackling and we hastily stepped back towards the bed when something burst in a spray of dirty sparks.

"It is out of control," she finally said, and I nodded and we agreed that it was imperative to call the fire brigade, and that's what we did, or rather what she did, with her cool and composed manner, one hand still on a hip as she explained the situation on the telephone. Then we waited in silence for the sirens and the firemen, the hoses and the sense of relief. But it was a long wait, too long, and my anxiety grew.

"The fire is dying down of its own accord," I said at last. "This means we have summoned the fire brigade for no good reason. I am embarrassed and I fear we will be accused of wasting their time. Clearly the blaze was not as bad as it seemed." And Isabel asked if I had any ideas about how to avoid looking like a fool or hoaxer when the firemen arrived to find only embers and fragments of exploded wine bottles cooling in lank grass, and I declared impetuously, "We must feed it."

Yes, that was the only answer. We had to add fuel, build the fire back up to its former glory, so there was something substantial for the firemen to put out when they turned up, so that everything would be in order and no one could be regarded as too easily panicked. I told Isabel that I would dismantle a table in the kitchen that we had never used, and throw it onto the sagging flames, and she nodded. I had screwed together the table only the previous month, but it had been a mistake, an item of furniture that we allowed to lurk there like a dreadful uncle.

But I struggled with the operation and the screwdriver kept slipping in my sweaty hand and the more I hurried the less efficient I became. Then I was overcome with an appalling thirst and I abandoned my task to pour a glass of water. As I glanced out of the window I saw Isabel on the garden path staggering under the weight of a bulging box. Reaching the fire, she relaxed her grip and the box tumbled onto the spitting embers and spilled its contents in an avalanche of white. Then she hurried back and I met her on the stairs. "What did you burn just now?"

She wiped her sooty forehead and grimaced at the same instant that I heard the distant sirens, and I associated this sound with her expression. A siren is a noise but it is also a mythic woman who entices a sailor to his doom. The sea was far away, yes, but I was a mariner on the waves of her disdain as she said, "Your love letters. I had to find something flammable in a hurry. All of them and the box I kept them in." And she shrugged and now the fire engine was coming up the lane and we rushed to the window again and saw that the flames were devouring the paper with abominable greed, and that they danced with joy as they did so, high and higher, even more ferocious now than earlier. An inferno.

The heat was so extreme that some of the letters were rising on pillars of shimmering air and taking off, unscathed, like scrawny birds, to roost in the rotten trees or flap down the lane over the heads of the firemen, one of whom suddenly reached out to snatch a page in mid flight. He drew it to him, unfolded it and read it, and as I watched him my cheeks began to burn too, as if they were part of the fire. This letter would incriminate me and I had no defence against the blazing passion of its prose, the deluded longing of its poetry, the flourish of my signature. It would be better not to even attempt to evade justice. I stepped out into the garden alone, arms raised in surrender, bound by ropes of smoke.

Dolly

YOU WANTED A HOUSE to live in, you were tired of the cramp and dampness, and I said I would help you. You imagined I was going to buy a house for you, despite the fact I had almost no money, because I gave off the wrong signals and made myself seem far more competent and influential than I really am. I should have said that I would *try* to help, rather than that I definitely would help, but it was too late to revise my promise and I was stuck with a task I couldn't manage.

Unfairly I blamed you, the eyes of pale green that were like the circles of the sky of very early dawn that showed through the portholes. Always you were awake first and peering at me when I woke up. The curly mass of auburn hair with honey streaks where the sun had spread his breakfast over you on the pillow. Living in a houseboat seemed like an adventure to me, but you regarded it as a nuisance. At night discarded bottles knocked against the hull like glass fists.

These were thrown off bridges by drunkards, poets or students returning home in the lulls between the rainclouds. The sluggish river was the same one that had flowed through novels and ballads for centuries and I enjoyed the way in which the currents nudged the barge. Rather like saying, "Remember I am here and I have seen so much in my life." But you thought that story was boring. You wanted a house that didn't sway when the winds blew. And I offered to provide.

One morning, strolling on dry land through narrow streets, I saw a building with a sign that declared, FREE HOUSE. An instant solution to my problem. But it was far too heavy for me to lift and take back to you, far too heavy for the barge. Also it was full of people, the same drunken men and women who disgorge rubbish from the bridges, and although I hugged the stones in an attempt to push it towards the riverbank, there were no offers of assistance from anyone there.

We live in a world of tricks and disappointments. The house might have been free but it came with conditions of weight and shape that made it impractical as a gift for you, and also it came with a tainted interior, with occupants disinclined to leave. There is no way I could have moved it down those narrow streets. So I bought a doll's house for you instead, one I saw in the window of an old shop, and I know this won't satisfy you, but my word will be kept in a smaller way.

Mengjie

MENGJIE IS A SCHOLAR and she offered to teach me something called *deep learning* and I made a joke about reading a textbook at the bottom of a coal mine. She laughed, the way she always laughs, with a resonance that vibrates every object in the room, and I waited for her to explain the real meaning to me. But no, she merely shook her head, took me by the arm and led me on a journey.

We vacated my office, still full of faintly humming furniture and machines, and a labyrinth swallowed us, the intersecting levels, stairways and corridors of the library, and before long I was passing into regions unknown, with her hand still on my arm, a hand that appears delicate but is capable of great strength. I was in her grip, heart and mind equally squeezed, hoping to be set free.

But not really wanting her to let me go, not just yet or ever. And as we penetrated the maze of knowledge, where shadows at the end of each long row of shelved books made me wonder if a minotaur was lurking, I turned over in my mind the words *deep learning* and asked myself if I understood them after all. Did they have something to do with artificial neural networks? I wasn't sure.

She led me into a chamber so thick with dust that the building itself seemed about to sneeze, and then she selected a book off a shelf and opened it under my nose. I saw that it was hollow, that the pages had been cut away to create a space in which rested a bottle, and that Mengjie had discovered this secret on her own. She urged me to pull out the cork and take a drink of the contents.

And I did so, because it was she who was asking me and no one else, and when I felt the liquid trickle down my throat I understood the geometry of the library, how it had grown organically over centuries, so that there were no maps of the paths through the rooms because it was all uncharted territory, a virgin book forest, yet I knew how to navigate my way among the complications.

"The bottle contains shallow learning, that's why," Mengjie explained, "and this shallow learning will help you find your way to deep learning, as it did for me." And she kept her hand on my arm but something had changed. When we left that space I was no longer following but guiding her. We parted a thick tapestry and found a door behind it and we entered a cavern of crystals.

But it was still a part of the library and full of books. And I selected a book so big that it took both of us to lift it from its adamantine shelf and lay it on the topaz floor, and I knew that this was the book of deep learning, the book that the book of shallow learning had led me to. And I licked my lips because they were shining among opals and sapphires and I asked Mengjie to help me.

We opened the volume together, but she said, "It is still your turn," and I knew I would have to climb onto the book, which also had pages cut away, but I managed this without trouble. The hollow space was so large that a man could fit easily inside it and I glanced at Mengjie for a clue and she nodded and I shut my eyes and jumped into the space, and I am still falling, still falling.

Elodie

IT'S A LONG WAY to Kinshasa from here, but not a long way from Kinshasa to elsewhere because just over the river is Brazzaville, and sometimes we stood in the park to look at the cafés on the far side, and occasionally we caught a boat across and sat at a table in one of those cafés and gazed curiously back.

Always watching the place where we didn't happen to be at that very moment. It was dangerous on both sides, but worse in the city where she lived, and especially perilous for me, conspicuous as I was, although I was with her and I spoke French and these things helped. Plus

I had my guitar close at all times and that reduced the tension because musical notes are like bullets of love sprayed in every direction that always strike the heart, and I played quite well.

She said to me, "We must leave soon" and she had been repeating this for months, years, and I nodded and agreed that we would. But we had nowhere to go, and I felt like a breaker of promises rather than a stranded engineer. Yes indeed, we could cross the river and come back, but we couldn't cross the sea. We weren't allowed to do that. The bureaucratic puzzles placed deliberately in front of us were too numerous, large, complex, and required too much money to solve.

Then I wondered if our identities might cross into each other and gaze back at the bodies they had left, and one night we sat on the edge of the bed and locked eyes and remained that way for hours and hours as the stars fell through the fumes outside and aromas of cooking and sounds of laughter drifted across the city. Then I found myself staring at myself as I was looking into a mirror, but I was lighter, more nimble, and I realised that we really had exchanged identities.

How would this help us escape together? It couldn't, and we fell into each other's arms, and I felt I was hugging myself tight but there was deep comfort in the contact. We had managed a feat that no one else had, but like an engineering project without a purpose, the end result was of no importance. Or was it? From my side of the river of identity I looked back at her, at Elodie, while she looked at me from her side. We had crossed the river of loneliness, the current that keeps people in their own shapes, and we were closer than before. That was our escape.

An escape into each other and back into ourselves. It is a long way from my heart to Elodie, but not a long way from Elodie to elsewhere. I play the guitar in the cooler light of dawn while we wait for the first ferry of the day to carry us over the flow and sometimes she is me and other times I am her, and we take turns standing in the park or sitting at café tables, man and woman, black and white, and the skeletal stumps of the bridge I was commissioned to build rust slowly.

Itxaso

YOU FLEW OUT OF the Basque lands one day and I asked myself what could possibly be the advantage of a glass aeroplane. You had designed it yourself but never explained why it was a good idea. You never even told me you were leaving. You took off while I was still in bed, buffeted by the turbulence of dreams, and you were already over the ocean when I finally opened my bleary eyes.

You were my favourite aviatrix. Itxaso, and I knew you would leave me before the year was out, because you simply had to fly far and keep flying, but I never expected it to happen without warning. When I heard the distant drone, I rushed to the flat roof of the house, trained the telescope on the sky and finally I saw you sitting up there on nothingness like a levitating woman. I gasped.

But it was the glass aeroplane that was carrying you away, every part transparent, even the engine and the fuel that fed it. You were headed towards South America, to Brazil or Argentina, I'm not sure what was on your mind or what you needed there or anywhere else. But I accepted it, I had no choice. And you continued to fly, exposed to the scrutiny of the elements and the angels.

What happened to you, Itxaso, on your voyage in that celestial window? Did you weave your way between waterspouts in the doldrums and did the fish caught in the spin of those vortexes mouth imprecations at you as you went past? I dreamed I was one of those fish, but I can no longer remember if my dream occurred before you left or the night after. My scales glisten like opals.

And you must glisten too, beaded with tiny rainbows, with the spray that washes your craft as the invisible propeller pulls you towards your destiny, and I drink wine as the stars come out, knowing that your brilliance is one of those stars up there, and I slowly and lovingly raise my glass in your general direction, although the aroma and gesture are too slow to ever reach you, Itxaso.

As I drink to your distant health and success

it suddenly seems to me that I know why your aeroplane had to be made of glass. You are wine too, Itxaso, and as oceans, mountains and jungle pass beneath you they are like the blue carpet, furniture and flowers that pass beneath my glass as I carry it out of the kitchen and into the garden. You are as heady as wine, as fierce yet mellow.

The whine of the engine, the wine of your soul.

Vanessa

SHE LIKES TO POUR water over me, especially when I am not prepared for it, although I soon begin to expect it all the time. She claims it is to remind me of my homeland, where it always rains. Vanessa, this thought is sweet but unnecessary, unlike you, who are sweet and essential, but the drenching of my entirety is still a joke to you and the sweetness that is part of you, and now I wish a few serious hours in which I may dry out. Will you give me those requested hours?

It was my own fault, because I bought the watering can for her, then afterwards I learned she lived in a house without a garden. What use is a watering can with no plants to water? There is a man to water as a substitute! The first time was from a high window when I was bending to tie an undone shoelace. I thought it was real rain and never looked up. As the weeks passed I became suspicious. It always seemed to rain on me but never on others in my vicinity. I palpitated.

Yes, palpitated in each drenching, in the repeated soakings, fearful I had offended the clouds, that those bulging fluffy balls of ominous darkness were conducting a vendetta against me, but one day I looked up and I saw her leaning over the balcony, tilting the watering can, and there were rainbows in the spray coming out of the spout, and she was the pot of golden smiles at the end of the rainbow, but I was at the other end, wet and harassed by the simulated precipitation.

I obtained an umbrella but it didn't help. We sit in the library, you and I, and my umbrella is open but you are under the purple canopy too, pouring the water over me in a steady stream. The same is true in any restaurant, in the cinema, or even at the airport and later on the flight itself. I sit and drip in my window seat as the mountains poke through the mist below, and you are next to me, Vanessa, watering me, a cloud above the other clouds, a noctilucent cloud, the highest cloud of all, shining at night like gossamer curls among the constellations.

You are turning me into a plant, Vanessa, and I already know that I am destined to become an orchid. One day when we no longer know each other I will be rooted to the floor and people will come and sniff me, pushing their noses into my bloom, my inflorescence, and emerge disappointed that I smell only of rain, not of beauty. What are the chances that one of those people will be you, unaware and as beautiful as ever and as mischievous, come to shower me with kisses like a hummingbird when I bend down to tie an undone root, an untangled tendril.

Zsuzsanna

I HAVE NEVER BEEN so depressed over a woman that I wished to kill myself. That seems an absurd course of action to me, for one thing it draws too much attention to oneself or what is left of oneself, the fading echoes of your life in the memories of those who knew you, it is a melodramatic gesture that the truly refined gentleman can only treat with derision. But after I met Zsuzsanna and bathed deeply in her melancholy, in the tangible darkness of her love, I decided to try it. Curiosity and symmetry were surely the two main motivations for the action I took.

Yes, Hungary still has one of the highest suicide rates in the world, but it is ranked only eighth. I have lived in countries with higher rates and with women more entropic and also during periods of my life when I felt even more unsuccessful than I did then, in that old apartment block in Budapest, in the Józsefváros district. But maybe I felt it would be a gift to Zsuzsanna, a way of paying tribute to her morbidity,

32

something that was more authentic than simply taking her for a picnic in a graveyard. The apartment block was twelve floors high and that is plenty.

But I still had doubts and if I threw myself from the top it would be too late on the way down to change my mind. I would hit the pavement and that would be that. Our apartment was on the first floor, the one above the ground floor, and it occurred to me that a fall from that altitude would not be fatal, that it would serve as a sample of the bigger end, that I could throw myself out of my own bedroom window twelve times instead of just once from the roof of the building and that these would be equivalent. So I opened the window and stepped through it.

You came back from work early, Zsuzsanna, with a bag of groceries, and caught me in the act after I had picked myself up from the pavement, dusted myself down, climbed the stairs to our apartment, reached the window and thrown myself out of it for a second time. You literally caught me. You dropped the bag, and the pastries and bottle of Tokaji inside were cracked but not destroyed, then you carried me tenderly in your arms back into the building and up the stairs and threw me out the window a third time. To teach me a lesson in melodrama.

This time the bottle was smashed when I landed on it and shards of glass cut my wrists and I bled to death. Not entirely to death, but exaggeration is part of the theatre of melancholy, the most flamboyant of all theatres. As I lay in that ungainly position and blood flowed from me, I remembered that waste is a sin and I reached inside the bag and plucked out the mangled pastries and crammed them in my mouth. The rich flodni, made from apples, walnuts and poppy seeds, filled the hole you left inside me, Zsuzsanna, with your lovely tangible darkness.

Peppiina

YOU WANTED TO CROSS the north pole in a balloon and when I objected to the adventure because of the risks, you pointed out that it wasn't so far from the north of Finland to the top of the world. Other people had tried it and failed. Both Andrée and Nobile had crashed and died on the ice, but you told me that those explorers didn't have what you had, which was a peculiar luck and an even stranger imagination. So I agreed to come with you, but you didn't want that, you told me that it would be better if I waited, sat on a sofa in a warm room somewhere, pining.

Pining for Peppiina, all I was good for, lacking the brain to be a navigator and the manual dexterity to be a mechanic, and I felt useless as always in your company, but you reminded me that soon I wouldn't be in your company, that you would be adrift over a world of crystalline whiteness, high above the pack ice, a woman of force and grace in the sky of bears, and that I shouldn't worry. Don't worry about anything at all and certainly not about everything, you said. We enjoyed a last sauna together on the island of Keskimmäinen Akusaari, your home.

Then I went to bed and steamed my dreaming mind while you inflated the balloon with hydrogen and at dawn you came to wake me up because it was ready. I rubbed at my eyes in disbelief when I saw it. I had expected something quirky, a balloon in the shape of a walrus, perhaps, but not this. Not a rhinoceros. It didn't fit any context, the reality of the environment, our latitude, the time of day, the stage our relationship had reached, but that was the point, you told me, stressing the word *point* and reluctantly I understood. The best form of defence is attack.

Balloons often burst. There are many malignant powers out there that love to pop them. Lightning strikes, the beaks of migrating birds, the propellers of aeroplanes and much more. On that island in the lake of Inarijärvi the gaseous beast strained at its mooring lines. A rhinoceros will charge first, will burst any threat with its horn before the threat has a chance to strike. Peppiina, you are clever, and I admire you vastly, but now I must wave you goodbye and cast you off, for although you are Finnish and our love is only halfway, your adventure has begun.

Insyirah

YOU WANTED ME TO design a house for you, so
we could live in it and watch the misty mountains
from the comfort of our veranda, and I agreed at
once, because for years I had wanted to put my
architectural skills to use. We were living with
your parents at the time, sharing that narrow
room at the top of their building with your sister
and her husband, and space was at a premium.
But I unrolled sheets of large paper, sharpened
my pencils and prepared to start work on the
project. And you, Insyirah, smiled at me when I
asked you to fetch me a ruler to help me draw the
lines, because there were no rulers to be had and
you brought an alternative.

You handed me a *kris*, a typical knife of your
people, and told me to use the blade as a ruler. I
unsheathed the weapon and my eyebrows rose on
my head, for the *kris* is not a straight-edged knife.
It has a wavy blade, very distinctive, very lethal
thanks to the wounds it will leave in a man or a
crocodile. And there, in that narrow room in the
north of Borneo, I tried to design a house that
was curves everywhere and I produced a result
that was bizarre to my eyes, but you loved it. You
said it had a special essence and in fact that was
why you had given me the *kris* to use as a ruler.
For these are not just weapons but also spiritual
objects, talismans.

This particular *kris* was a *pusaka*, a magical
heirloom passed down through many generations

36

of your family from the time of Makhdum Karim and the founding of the Sultanate of Sulu and it was saturated with good fortune. Our new house would be an inspiration, you said, with Mount Kinabalu facing us every night as we rocked on our love swing, and yes, Insyirah, I would rock you to sleep later in my arms, and the *kris* would hang sheathed above our bed, a gift from your family. And softly I would walk across the wavy floor and enter the wavy kitchen to make for myself a wavy glass of hot frothy tea adorned with a wavy sea of bubbles.

Jimena

USED TO SLEEPING IN the jungle, often just in a hammock strung between two trees with a tarpaulin to keep the rain off, Jimena agreed to my proposal to go camping on the weekend without even having to think about it for a moment. It was a reflex for her to say yes, and so off we went into the forest but we chose a spot where we could look down on the sea between the trees. We erected the tent and then gathered twigs for a small fire and cooked beans and chillies in one pot and made coffee in another, and although the food was burnt and the drink smoky they tasted marvellous, for it had been a long hard hike to reach our destination.

The sun went down and in the twilight she told me tales about Costa Rica and the ghosts that inhabit the lonely places, but they were almost the same as the ghosts that inhabit anywhere else, so I felt myself nodding off. Then she suggested we go to bed and I unrolled the two sleeping bags and crawled into the tent with them. She told me she had never slept in a sleeping bag before and when she had wriggled inside hers it was true that she looked like a caterpillar, as the moon rose and gleamed on the fabric of the tent and illuminated the interior. We lay side by side but I was motionless while she kept squirming, undulating her strong body.

She was enjoying the fact she resembled a caterpillar and this was an enjoyment it was impossible for me to deny her. I had no right to ask her to desist from trying to be a caterpillar. Little did I know that she always succeeded at everything she attempted. That's one special thing about Jimena, she was utterly convincing, to the extent that a whim was also a wish, and a wish was a promise to herself, one she intended to keep. And she kept this one. I fell asleep despite the fact she was still wriggling, because I was weary from the day's exertions, but I woke in the middle of the night feeling cold and I saw that my sleeping bag had disappeared.

It had been eaten from around me. Jimena in her own sleeping bag had devoured it. One doesn't stay a caterpillar forever. The flap of the tent was open and moonlight was streaming in and then a dark shape crossed the moon. But it wasn't dark in itself, it was pale and fragile.

Eurema albula, the ghost yellow, a butterfly found throughout Central America, a huge specimen, a phantasmagoric sight I couldn't blink away and didn't want to, because I knew that Jimena had transformed herself like a character in one of the magic tales she had told, from a woman into this graceful flying being, and I laughed and sobbed at the same time until dawn.

Flutura

YOU DON'T BELONG TO my past or even my present, like so many others, but to the time that is yet to come, and this marks you out as different. Also your voice, which I have heard despite the distance that separates us, not over the telephone, not in my dreams, but in the voice of a famous actress, who you claim sounds just like you, and yes, it's an unusual voice, also marks you out as different. And your similarities in other ways to very distinctive people, your hair and eyes and frown, which are like the hair, eyes and frowns of other actresses specified by you in your numerous letters, mark you out as different, if not unique. You like to send me letters the old-fashioned way, sealed in envelopes and written on pale green paper. You say that in the future everyone will go back to writing letters exactly like these, and you told me this in one of the letters, the most recent letter in fact, and I believe you.

I prefer to believe people who exist in the future because even if they are wrong it can never be said that any harm has yet been done. I will meet you soon, I will pull in the future towards the present, while simultaneously I move with the present forwards and in the middle that's where you will be, you and me. At least if all goes to plan. It's a plan that could fall apart at many stages of its implementation, especially in winter. I am required to cross the *Bjeshkët e Nemuna,* the Accursed Mountains, and how deep might the snows be? I don't yet know, because that's a future event, which means you should know, and yet you mentioned nothing in your letters, so presumably there will be no insurmountable obstacles for me among those peaks. My pockets will be full of your letters anyway and if I am stranded I can always burn them for emergency heat after I have carefully memorised every one.

The smoke will rise up and cover everything and you will come to me from out of it, a wreathed woman like an embodied anticipation, and it will occur to me as I try to warm my frozen hands on the embers of the margins that the letters *are* you, that they contain all I know about you, and that to incinerate them is to force you to assume the form of a real woman. You will be scorched out of ink into reality. There will be only one problem, the problem of scale. In the letters you fit my imagination exactly and it is an imagination shaped like the kinds of women I have known, but in fact you are a gigantic figure,

40

much too big for my mind and heart. Flutura, your face on the skyline is as huge as the face of those actresses on the silver screen, your voice as loud, and I am reduced to the role of a spectator, a patron of the cinema, one who has waited for this film and already wonders about a sequel.

Cyrine

SITTING ON A RUINED WALL in Sbeitla, she dangles her legs and asks me to remove her shoes and put her slippers on. Her feet are at the same level as my face. Cyrine, you are not at home now! But she doesn't care about that. She wants to wear her slippers, which are in the bottom of her bag, which is slung over my shoulder. It is a heavy bag but I have agreed to carry it for her all the way. How far is that? How far is all the way?

I don't know, but I hope to find out, if not today, if not next week, or next month, next year, then certainly before I die, if we are still together in the future. I estimate that all the way is further than the distance that we have already come but I can't be sure. Even Cyrine is unable to offer an assurance on this matter. We will have to wait and see. I unlace her shoes and take them off. Her feet are a little swollen, as are mine, and I blow gently on them to cool them.

Then I lower her bag to the ground, open it and rummage inside. I can't feel the slippers. There are too many other objects in the way that I must unpack first. I reach inside and pull them out. Sunglasses, lipstick, combs, perfume, a file for her nails, bottles of lotion for her skin, a jar of vitamins, an electric fan, packet of mints, tweezers for her eyebrows.

Beneath these are items I regard as more practical and of which I approve. A map, a compass, a bottle of water, a length of string, a knife, a box of matches, a whistle, a bag of dried figs. I continue to rummage and remove. There's a long way to go before I reach the slippers. And some surprises in store.

Cyrine, what possessed you to pack a table lamp in your bag? It is useless here in the ancient wilderness where only the ruins stand and stand not very well. But I have misjudged her. For in the bag is also a generator to provide power to make it work, a table on which to stand it, and a large book to read by its light. And two chairs to be arranged around the table. And dinner plates and cutlery. But how can we cook food without pots and pans? That's the mystery now.

Oh I see, there are cooking utensils in the bag too. A large saucepan. A large pot. There is also a gas cooker and a large gas cylinder to feed it. And a vase of flowers to help create a nice atmosphere. And a sink with running taps to wash the dirty dishes afterwards, and a reservoir to provide water for the taps. How did you manage to fold an artificial lake into such a modest bag, Cyrine?

There are boats on the lake and people on

them. But these aren't the only humans in the bag. There is a chef to cook our food, a waiter to serve it, and a musician with a violin to play melodies while we eat. There is also a restaurant critic who will write a piece for his newspaper about the quality of the experience. And now finally I locate the slippers at the bottom of the bag and I slip them smoothly on your feet while you wriggle your toes in pleasure. And the boats pull into shore and the passengers climb out, carrying their own tables and chairs, and thus the restaurant grows around us, and we feel inadequately dressed for the occasion, too casual, you in your slippers and me in my desert boots, filthy with the dust of Sbeitla.

Amivi

WE ARE IN A CANOE, you and I, somewhere in East Timor and we are paddling up a fast river, so our arms are working hard and our muscles are aching, but there is no alternative, we must keep going. The waterfall is ahead of us, I can hear it now in the distance above the rushing of the current, and I grit my teeth and try even harder to propel us against the flow.

You told me about a cave behind the waterfall where there is a pot of gold. I believed you because I have never known you to lie. The gold was hidden there during the war and nobody ever came to claim it. Now we are setting out to

43

take it for ourselves, because that is within the bounds of morality, we have been told so by our consciences, which we examined.

All of us should examine our consciences from time to time. It's not easy but it's essential. We often go through life without examining our consciences. That is not a good thing. Anyway, our consciences passed the exam. What ought to be said about this? Congratulations to our consciences! And now the graduation ceremony is taking place, the canoe voyage up this river to a pot of hidden gold.

"The money will reverse the decline in our fortunes," you said to me and the idea of such a reversal instantly appealed. Reversals are not just negative. They can be inspiring, beneficial, indispensable. We crave to reverse our decay, our regression, our slide into practical difficulties and abstract despair. Reversal is a pleasing word in our ears, a musical mantra.

And now something odd occurs. A fish passes us in the wrong direction and it is swimming backwards. All the fish that we have seen so far have come from upstream, from the direction of the waterfall, not from behind us. And the canoe is no longer difficult to paddle. The current has changed direction, or maybe it is the minutes and seconds that have done that.

Yes, time itself has gone into reverse. We rush forward without effort. Turn a final bend in the river. And the waterfall sparkles before us, high and thin, and it is falling upward, against the pull of gravity. We prayed too hard for reversal in our lives, Amivi, and now we must accept the penalty. To go backward while going forward, thus our prayers are answered.

It all happens too fast. No chance for us to jump through the ribbon of water and land in the cave mouth as our canoe is sucked into the sky. Up we go, to the top of the waterfall, where a rainbow waits, and as we collide with the spectrum we both instantly understand that we are the gold we seek, but still hidden in the dark of the inaccessible recesses of our hearts.

Charlotte

IT WAS HOT, much too hot, and there was nothing cold to drink in the house. Even the water in the bottles in the fridge was lukewarm. Charlotte said to me, "We need a freezer, if we don't install one soon we will expire." And although this was an exaggeration, I didn't dispute it, because it served my purpose too. I was hot, as hot as she was, and she was as hot as the desert outside, the desert that stretched into the limitless west, a desert full of kangaroo bones that had not been carved into flutes and probably never would be.

I left the house and climbed into my car and I was baking and my shirt was a different colour now. The sweat had turned it from pale yellow to dark grey and vapour came off it, so it appeared I was wearing a cooling pancake draped over my body instead of a cotton garment. I drove hotly to the centre of the hot town and entered a hot shop and bought a freezer, right there and then, and packed it in the car and drove back, and staggered with it into the house, and plugged it in and then jammed it with bottles of water.

When I first opened the door, before the interior had been given a chance to grow cold, I was surprised to see a landscape within, a landscape identical to the one outside the windows. A desert scene. The freezer seemed too small a space for a desert to exist inside it, but that's what it contained and I didn't question it because I was too hot for questions and too hot for answers. I just wanted a cold drink. Charlotte and I waited impatiently and after only one hour we went into the kitchen and opened the freezer door again. This time the landscape that greeted us was a temperate one, with forests of oaks and elms undulating into the distance, and although the water in the bottles was cool, it wasn't cold. So we closed the freezer door and waited another hour, twiddling our thumbs on the unbearable sofa, unbearable because it was so hot and also because the colour scheme was dreadful. Then we went to check again and this time the freezer revealed a desolate vista of snow and ice. But the water had frozen and shattered the glass bottles.

One or two bottles further away had survived. I had to climb into the freezer in order to retrieve them. It was a long way. I don't know how it happened but suddenly the door closed

46

behind me and the light went off. Charlotte, was it one of your unpleasant jokes or was it a genuine accident? Luckily the *aurora australis* provided enough illumination to enable me to see. I took the unbroken bottles in my hands and began the journey home the long way. I knew I wouldn't be able to open the heavy freezer door from inside. I set off in the direction of the low sun, towards the warmer lands, and then beyond them to the torrid realm, the country where I have made my home with the woman who likes to shut me in the freezer, or who at the very least doesn't care too much if the door slams accidentally behind me or not. I suspect she sits on the sofa now, hot Charlotte, her eyes gazing out of the window, waiting to see that speck on the horizon that will be me, coming across the desert with the water that is cold no longer, that will need to be chilled again.

Arabella

"I OWN A COIN that always comes back to me, no matter how often I spend it."

"I bet you don't!"

"Very well, let's bet on it."

"Such things are impossible," I say.

"You are right."

Arabella hands me a coin, the coin she lost in the bet. I put it in my pocket. Arabella hands me a coin, the coin she won in the bet.

47

Oksana/Ksenya

TWIN SISTERS AND I always found it difficult or even impossible to tell them apart and they exploited the situation for the sake of humour, but the joke was always on me and though I didn't mind at first, because it was fun, at the end of the relationship the game began to disturb me a little. Only one of them was supposed to be my lover, not both, and yes that's how it was, but I never knew which one I was kissing at any moment.

The concept of 'one' in this situation was made of two parts, two women, a pair of identical sisters, and only on those rare occasions when I saw them together was I able to separate them in my mind. And yes, I looked for differences, tiny details in order to distinguish them, but it was futile, for truly they were perfect mirror images.

Это ты. Он я.

And I stood in front of the mirror in the hallway, the long mirror in the gloom of the winter light, and I wondered what they saw when they did the same thing. Did they see themselves in the silvered glass or did they see each other? Could they face each other and mimic the gestures of the other and thus make mirrors redundant? Why then was there a mirror in this lonely house that we shared on the isolated steppe? A long mirror in a silver frame.

Это мы. Кто мы?

I walked slowly towards the mirror, utterly determined to remove it from the wall, to take it away. And that's how I learned that I too was one of a twin, that I had a brother who was identical to me in every way. There was no mirror on the wall. It was my brother who stood there and he was peering at me intently, combing his slick hair and adjusting a sombre tie.

We have adapted to the environment in which we find ourselves. We sit at a table and play cards and drink vodka to make the seasons pass quickly. I wonder what else has a twin. When the game is over I stand at the open door and stare through the blizzard at another house that appears now and then when the lightning flashes. If only I could be certain now that I was me, that you are you, that she is you, and that he is me. That we are they.

48

Tabarak

THE PYRAMIDS HAVE already lasted for millennia and they will last for many more, and when I ask Tabarak why they have proved to be so sturdy, she says, "The answer to that question is simple. If a high building falls down, what shape does it take? It becomes a mound of rubble, yes? And that rubble is pyramidal. A pyramid can't really fall down because it is already in the shape of a building that has fallen down."

This is why pyramids are difficult to destroy. I remember her words and the following day when I strike my leg on a corner of one of the low tables in the living room. I limp to a chair and ask her, "Why do we have so much furniture? It's almost like the clutter to be found in an ancient tomb. Is that the look you are aiming for?" But she wraps my injury in bandages without replying. I don't press the point. Tabarak is a woman who can't be made to answer when she simply doesn't want to.

Next morning I fall out of bed. I had been thrashing all night because of dreams that were very peculiar, nightmares unlike any I have experienced before. In the light of dawn I roll off the mattress and land on the floor and I damage my arm. I wake up instantly and wail, and Tabarak wakes and tends to me, her smooth voice comforting as she bandages my forearm and elbow. But I can't get back to sleep. I limp into the kitchen to prepare breakfast for us both. Then

I spill a pan of boiling water all over myself and my abdomen needs to be bandaged. Tabarak does this with beautiful efficiency.

I guess I ought to mention that one of the bookcases topples onto me in the afternoon. I am unable to leave the house because of my injuries and it's boring just sitting there, so I decide to read a book. The one I want is on the highest shelf. I reach for it and pull, but it is stuck and the entire bookcase is falling and I have no time to evade it. Books tumble out and strike me on my body, and one particularly large and heavy volume on Egyptian history lands on my skull and knocks me unconscious.

When I recover my senses, I am sitting in my favourite chair, which is as large as a throne, and Tabarak is applying the final bandage. There is no part of me that is unwrapped, I am bandaged from head to foot. I'm unable to stir from my perch on that chair, which I now remember was bought by her as a present for me. She has clearly thought ahead. She leaves and locks the front door behind her and steps out into the sun and the world of palm fronds, and I am left alone to wait for an archaeologist.

Years, decades, centuries pass. The house collapses around me, caves in, and I am at the heart of it, surrounded by my treasure, all the furniture that accumulated during our relationship. The shape of the collapse is pyramidal. If only Tabarak would enrol on an archaeology course, secure a position as leader of an expedition, come back to dig me out! But she won't. She is not the kind of woman who can be made to discover an unknown pharaoh if she doesn't want to. My fate, my tomb, sealed.

Eilah

THE FRUIT FLIES in my room are strange beings. They ignore the fruit in the bowl and like to hang around the onions instead, which is fine by me, but why call yourself a fruit fly if you are going to do that? That's like calling yourself a housefly while only living in a tent, or calling yourself a hermit crab while being a bigshot in crab society.

Eilah can't understand why I get so annoyed about this. They are fruit flies as far as she's concerned, even if they seem to prefer onions, and to make a fuss about it is pointless. We go out together into the balmy night to cool off, but cooling off in a balmy night isn't easy, unless you splash in public fountains, and no one does that here, and neither do we. The law is strict on anarchic displays. Towers blot out the stars with bright lights and immense bulk.

We stroll among them. Then I understand something, while we are walking together, she and I, but not holding hands because that is frowned on here. I call myself a human being but what precisely am I being? I am a human being what? A human being a fruit fly. A human being a hermit crab. I am just as bad as those creatures

51

who call themselves one thing but act like another. For I am a human being a philosophical worrier, yet I never describe myself in that way. I have learned a valuable lesson.

Eilah is a teacher and I have found instruction in her presence, this hot night in Singapore as we wait for the traffic lights to change before daring to cross the road, even though there's no traffic in sight, and I decide that I will stop worrying, that if those insects prefer onions that is none of my business, and now we pass an all-night café and we enter on impulse and drink coffee while facing each other. And in whispers I call her names as sweet as the sugar that dissolves in the cups.

Aleksandra

I SPRINKLE NORMAL TABLE SALT on my food, but Aleksandra tells me this isn't good enough, that it's not as healthy as sea salt. She should know because she is from Sečovlje, that town in Slovenia famous for its saltpans.

As the sea comes in, it floods the pans, then it is allowed to evaporate in the sun, and what it leaves behind is the finest salt in the world. That is what I am led to believe, but naturally I just smirk. "I intend to stick with my table salt," is my reply while she shakes her chestnut hair so that it wafts my meal, the meal to which I am adding salt while I speak, a dinner of green leafy vegetables and red peppers.

It's true that Slovenia is one of the very few Slavic countries that understands the meaning of a salad and accepts that the concept has a valid right to exist as a real object. I've already added olive oil. And now I'm adding salt, but Aleksandra takes me by the arm, pulls me up from the table and says:

"Don't you have any idea how table salt is made? I will show you?" And I don't resist, the touch of her hand on my wrist is too pleasing, so I allow her to take me out of the house, through a maze of cobbled streets, to a warehouse in a part of the town I have never visited before. "This is a table salt factory."

I wonder why a town so famous for excellent sea salt would have such a factory in its territory, but Aleksandra explains that it's much cheaper to make table salt, that the export markets demand low prices, and with her foot she nudges open the wooden door a little and I peer through a crack into the interior of the building. I'm amazed.

A man with bulging muscles and a sledgehammer is breaking tables, smashing them to tiny bits, pounding the bits to grains, and the grains to dust. Another man is shovelling up the dust and pouring it into cardboard packets that will be sold in the supermarkets.

Now I know why furniture shops are only full of new tables, never old ones, and I appreciate why I have such a wooden taste in my mouth always. She leads me back to my salad but my appetite has gone. Vanished, varnished. Food is meant to be put on tables, not tables put on food. Ah well!

Simone

THE AERODROME is a small establishment with a building for the controller and one hangar for the planes. I went to visit Simone every morning on my bicycle while the coconut trees swayed on the edges of the road. Now I knew a typhoon was coming. The aerodrome would be closed until after the storm had passed. Simone was in the control tower and she waved at me through the windows and I turned from the road onto the runway and I stopped pedalling and allowed the wind to push me. My shirt undulated as it did so and made a flapping noise.

"Another windsock is missing," she said, as she came down the tight spiral stairs from the tower to the runway. "The wind keeps stealing them and leaving an unadorned pole behind."

"That's not seemly," I replied, and I clucked my tongue to express my consternation. A windsock shows force and direction of wind at a glance and without one, the aerodrome controller, who is a meteorologist as well as a radio operator and aviation expert, is forced to lick a finger, hold it up high and rotate it, to evaluate the sensation of chill and thereby judge those two qualities of the currents of air.

"Let me have your shirt," she continued blithely. And that's how my favourite shirt, the most colourful piece of fabric I have ever owned, became a substitute windsock.

Then the coconut trees started groaning so loudly that we took refuge inside the concrete control tower, in a storeroom without windows, and we huddled down and waited and in the light of a dim electric lamp we told stories to each other, while doors slammed somewhere far away, in some distant town, and dogs flew through the sky, tails still wagging madly.

When it was over and we emerged, we found that the hangar door had been staved in and that the light aircraft inside were all on their backs, but that my shirt was still in place, now dangling limply from the pole. "It is too colourful for the wind's sense of style," Simone offered. I climbed the pole, slippery with huge drops of tropical rain, and retrieved it, washed to perfection and dried crisply, and I wore it proudly but not proudly enough because Simone regarded me with dismay.

"If it doesn't suit a typhoon, it must suit a tycoon instead, so how can it suit you? This is all highly improbable."

On each subsequent visit to the aerodrome I found a different example of gentlemanly attire attached to the pole. First a pair of boots, very large indeed. Then enormous trousers. I understood what was happening. After millions of years of nakedness the wind in this region, on this tiny island, had decided to dress itself like a metropolitan breeze. Windsocks without the rest were absurd and gauche. Who walks around nude but in socks? It was beneath this wind's dignity. And yet—

My shirt wasn't good enough for it, my favourite shirt. Rejected by a storm that clearly prefers to blow bare-chested across the coral islands and reefs, it now sagged on my body like a sack for weary cheeks and so I hung it in its own hangar, in the wardrobe of my bedroom in my house in the town, among the tiny aircraft that stand on the shelves for ties, and forgot about it, while those perfectly crafted models waited in vain for an oblivious Simone to give them clearance for takeoff. And the wind takes the boots and trousers without saying thanks.

Eleftheria

THE ISLAND OF HYPEREIA is one of those locations that have been lost in the past three thousand years, thus we believed ourselves justified to point to a random island and say, "There it is," without fear of contradiction. And it wasn't even a real island but a small hill that stood in the rain, and when the rain stopped and the sun broke through the clouds the damp ground around the hill reflected the sky just as a calm sea does, then the puddles began steaming and shrouded the island in mist, making it more mysterious, and we knew for sure.

"Let's cross over and explore it," said Eleftheria, but I wondered aloud how we might do that without a boat, and she laughed and ran through the water and the mist, and I followed her. Our shoes were boats. That's one way of looking at it, a nicer way than acknowledging that the water was very shallow, only a centimetre deep, and draining away already. Our shoes were boats and the laces were the rigging and the tongues were sails or perhaps they were the tongues of thirsty and tired sailors drooling in anticipation of reaching shore.

The island was a hill, yes indeed, and a rocky limestone outcrop at that and riddled with caves, and because riddles have always baffled me I fell behind and Eleftheria went ahead and she peered into the mouth of the largest cave and said, "He is at home," and I wondered who she was referring to, but then I remembered the most famous inhabitant of Hypereia and I nodded and lowered my voice. "Maybe we ought to come away now." But she dismissed my fears and waited for me to catch up with her and gaze into that humid darkness until my eyes adjusted and I saw him in the far corner, asleep with a boulder for a pillow.

"We are safe," Eleftheria told me, "because he is enjoying twenty winks."

This was logical enough. A person with two eyes requires forty winks as the minimum number to act as a refreshing sleep. While he, the lonely brooder of Hypereia, never the same since Odysseus came to visit, requires only half that total. His snoring was like the rasp of tectonic plates rubbing against each other far below the sea, but the sea we had crossed had no great depth and indeed it had almost dried up already. How would our shoes manage to float back to safety without scraping their hulls to fragments? For our shoes, yes our shoes, are boats.

Lisandra

SHE PLAYED THE DRUMS in an Afro-Cuban music club every weekend and it was her obsession as well as a job. I went a few times to watch her do her thing with the bongos and the congas and other drums with names I never learned, and the way her hands moved on the taut skins was a sight more astonishing to me than to the audience, because it was something without a parallel in our domestic life. At least that was true back then, before the changes took place, an alteration in the rhythm of our relationship, in the tempo and timbre of our conjugal bliss.

Lisandra began to want everything to be music, to be sultry, complex, trancelike, accumulative and physical. This was good, it was invigorating, exciting, uplifting. But some things just aren't like music and can't stand being forced to compare with it. Cooking, yes, that's fine, the tapping of a spoon against the side of the stirred pot, the clack of the knife as it chops the vegetables on the wooden board, the spitting of the oil and the hissing of the steam, these all have a musical element or at least can be regarded as pulsations, expressions of a drumbeat.

But how does paying the rent equate to music, or unblocking the sink, or taking out the trash? If those things are music, they are bad tunes and a man who dances to them is an imbecile. And sleep is surely the opposite of music, it's a prolonged rest, and a rest on a musical score is a sign that a note mustn't be played, that a musician must desist from making noise, that the rest of the melody is enhanced and justified by the pause. But yes, it seems that Lisandra was too zestful, too full of time signatures, minims and syncopation, too in cahoots with her art.

She started playing the drums on random objects throughout the house and not just on pots and pans and table tops but on any available surface, even on the meniscus of the flooded sink, the tottering pile of unpaid bills in brown envelopes, the mounds of discarded rinds and peels waiting to be thrown out. And I knew that she was going to drum on my sleep too. I woke in the middle of the night, sweating profusely, flat on my back, and she was playing my knees, beating intricate and possibly even sacred and secret rhythms on the cartilage of my caps.

When life becomes a drum, we must decide to stick it out or leave. In the end, although I loved her deeply, I was too bruised to continue. I had to say farewell to her, to her vibrancy, her exquisite sense of timing, to all the pains in my joints and my skull. As I walked away from the house, it was impossible for me not to look back. She had climbed on the roof and was playing it and everything in all the rooms was jumping and breaking, but not my heart, which was still inside the cage of my ribs, where I keep it because it's wild and much safer locked up.

Thérèse

AS WE CAME BACK and reached the door, Thérèse declared, "It's the wrong key," and I was surprised by this and cried, "Really?" and she replied in a voice of anguish, "I don't know, but it might be." It was one of those rare anguished voices that are hushed and conspiratorial and philosophical too and it caught me up and propelled me along. And that's how it started, the strange night that led to stranger days.

I said, "Perhaps it's the right key, but the lock is wrong," and this was a definite possibility, and to test it she pushed the key into the lock and it fitted, so then she said, "The lock is right but maybe it's the wrong door," but I looked carefully at the door and stroked it with my hands and shook my head. "It's the right door, for sure, but it could be the case that it's the wrong house." And she nodded at this.

There was one way to find out. She turned the key and gently pushed the door and it opened and we went inside and explored the rooms for an hour. "It's the right house," Thérèse announced, "but I wouldn't place a bet on it being the right town." And I was forced to agree with her that if the town was wrong, then the value of this house being the right one was diminished by a considerable amount…

So we left the house and locked the front door and went for a wander around the town, and we finally had to conclude, as we came back to our house, that it was actually the right town. But something still nagged us, wouldn't let us rest, and it occurred to both of us simultaneously that just because a town is the right one, it doesn't follow it's in the right country. Our investigation needed to be thorough.

And so we toured on foot this country of ours, of hers I should rather say, because I was a stranger and Thérèse was a native, and although it is a small country, Luxembourg in fact, it was still big enough to take many weeks to inspect its corners, its hills, ravines and forests, the villages and castles, and when we eventually returned to our house I really hoped the ordeal was over, that we could go to bed.

But Thérèse sighed, "Yes, it's the right country, that has been proven beyond doubt, but do we know if it's the right—" And I tried to anticipate what she planned to say, to finish her sentence for her. "Right continent?" I asked, but she shook her head. "Planet," she announced, and in my chest my heart sank and it kept sinking, and I bent over, not to pick it up but to retie my shoelaces tighter for the journey.

Olivia

SHE FELT IT WAS IMPORTANT to reduce our power consumption, both for fiscal and environmental reasons, and I agreed with her, and yes, the burning of fossil fuels is a deplorable way of generating energy, especially in a place like this where there is so much sunlight.

Solar cells are the answer, and it was with excessive joy that she returned one evening with a basket full of lamps that stored sunlight and gave it back out at night. And we arranged them around the house and the garden.

The sun went down and darkness drew over us and the lamps came on automatically, because that's what they are designed to do, they recharge themselves during the day when the bright sun shines on them, and when night comes they feed that power into their bulbs.

Daylight turns them off but their own light isn't strong enough to do that. The inside of our house was suddenly illuminated in every room and the garden was flooded with light too, the solar-powered lamps balanced on every available surface or even on top of other objects, like squat metallic and glass insects, like big and extra radiant robotic glow-worms.

Olivia smiled in the glare and that was the afterimage that was burned on my retina afterward, her face just like it would be in a photograph that had been taken without her permission by a newspaper reporter. Because we had overlooked something. There were too many lamps clustered near each other. The combined shine was bright enough to trigger the switches in the lamps and turn them off. They thought it was day again. So the first time they shone for us, it was just a flash.

We blinked and they blinked too and went out. But the moment it was dark again, they came back on, and then had to turn themselves off. And so on. I was dazzled by the furious flickering, hypnotized even. It was too fast, too frantic, hectic, mesmeric. I wanted them to stop, I wanted to kill the power, but there was no master switch. All were independent sources of energy, each had stored sunlight within itself and now intended to flash it out in intense bursts that threatened to fry our minds, Olivia's and mine, and rupture our eyeballs like hot grapes.

Our house became an insane lighthouse stranded inland and we were a pair of frozen figureheads, rooted to the spot, capable of only the smallest gestures, like mannequins in a world of stroboscopes, and I knew that our brains were being randomly reprogrammed by the tempo of this incessant flip from dazzle to darkness and back. I never believed we would make it to dawn alive, but that turned out not to be necessary, for halfway through the night the flashing stopped, abruptly, and all the lamps remained on. It was now possible for our eyes to slowly cool in a steady glow. The power levels of the lamps had dipped continuously and finally reached the stage where they weren't bright enough in combination to fool any of them into thinking day had come. So they stayed on.

But Olivia, I still see you as if you are a photograph of a woman, not the woman before me, with that startled smile, that moment captured as a branded image in my mind, your long hair bleached by the ferocity of the first pulsation of light, your high cheekbones glaring and nostrils stark as craters on the moon, an unfair image because it says nothing at all about the real you, and you say the same about me.

Anahita

WE ENDED UP by having a discussion about ghosts, I don't know why, and I told her that although I didn't believe in ghosts I had nonetheless had an eerie experience that certainly could be called a personal ghost story, but it was nothing special in the telling. And she demanded that I tell it, and I explained that once in a pub with some friends an empty table had flipped itself upside down, which maybe doesn't sound that impressive, but with a weary nod of his head the barman had said, "The ghost is early tonight, he must be in a hurry," and we all nodded too, as if this explanation was the most natural one, and only later, when we were outside, did we pause in our tracks and ask each other, "Did that really occur?" And the aspect I recall most vividly is that when the incident was happening there was no feeling of astonishment. Only afterwards.

Anahita said firmly, "There are no such things as ghosts." Her culture and religion had no room for the concept. The souls of dead people never remain down here, on Earth, but are compelled to rush off to paradise or perdition. I told her, "Maybe it wasn't a ghost that moved that table, it is perfectly feasible that it was a trick or an effect of electromagnetism or a freak indoor breeze that was the cause, I don't know, but the barman told us it was a ghost and none of us cared to dispute that *at the time*." And it was very important to me to stress how normal everything had seemed at the moment it happened, how I had seen it from the corner of my eye and had only shrugged and carried on drinking. But none of us were drunk, it was essential to stress that too. She said:

"My father loved gardening, it was his passion, and once in our house in Tehran when I was very small he was walking slowly among the roses at the bottom of the garden when he heard a rustling and a laugh. He saw a large round yellow face peering at him from the bushes and it continued to laugh and then it told him that it was all that remained of his uncle, the uncle who had passed away the previous month. My father threatened the face with a stick he carried. He knew it wasn't his uncle at all. The yellow face retreated into the bushes and vanished."

Anahita brought me milky coffee and dishes of cashew nuts, apricots and grapes on a silver tray. She liked these traditional gestures. I thought about her story and her faraway garden, now lost, and said, "Whose ghost was it then?" and she repeated her assertion, "There are no ghosts. It was just a *djinn* in the garden." And I said, "A genie, you mean?" She nodded and added, "There are never ghosts, there are only genies pretending to be ghosts." And I wondered why they did that, but she only smiled and then I wondered why any of us did anything, why for instance I now raised my coffee to lips that still tasted of ghost story.

Misaki

ONE OF MY FRIENDS called me on the telephone to describe a nightmare she had. I hate nightmares but I haven't had a proper one for many years. When I was about twenty years old I had a nightmare so bad that it used up my entire lifetime's supply of them, the same way a lost explorer drinks up all his water and eats all his rations and there is nothing left, and that's really what seems to have happened with my dream life. I have never had a nightmare since and I don't want one, not like that one. I dreamed I was married to a girl with a porcelain head.

She was very sad because her head was porcelain and everybody laughed at her behind her back, which was flesh, and maybe if she had been porcelain all over, her head wouldn't have been so bad, it wouldn't have been so obtrusive and ugly. And it really was ugly even though it was beautiful. I mean that it was a beautiful object in itself but the need to wear a porcelain head instead of a real one is a grotesque fact and such facts are ugly. I had a horrid and perverse urge to lightly but mockingly tap her head with a teaspoon, which I resisted.

I felt acutely sorry for her but I was also embarrassed to be in her company and I felt bad that I wasn't more supportive. I decided to take her to the cinema, but to my horror the random film we went to see turned out to be a documentary about people with porcelain heads. The documentary revealed that the first people to be given such heads were soldiers in the trenches in the First World War who had lost their heads in explosions. The first heads were very crude, without faces, just big ceramic balls, but the doctors carried on improving the methods and eventually they invented porcelain heads with expressions. I stole a sly glance at my spouse to see how she was taking it and she was weeping tears of blown glass.

But I also noticed that she had a crack in her head above her ear and that wires and tendrils were poking out of it, and I knew that this was where her handle should be but that it was missing, probably broken off in a fall. I felt disgusted, and angry at myself for my disgust, and disgusted at my anger, and I also knew that asking her for a divorce would make her head break open completely but I really didn't want to stay with a woman who had a porcelain head. The horror of the nightmare was a blend of the fact she had lost her original head in an accident that we never talked about and also that I was stuck in a relationship with a woman without a real head. Although it sounds very silly the dream was in fact acutely disturbing. The sadness of it was too intense, the sadness was a big part of the horror, it was a cosmic sadness, infinite and appallingly cruel, fundamentally unbearable.

And then I woke up, or she woke up, or we both woke up, or neither of us did. I still don't really know and I doubt I ever will.

Marguerite

MARGUERITE FROM CAMEROON said, "No sex before marriage!" and meant it and I respected her wishes, but sleeping together and not doing anything turned out to be beyond us. She liked to quote the Bible and pray before bedtime, but her body was lithe and strong and embedded in the physical world, despite the best intentions of her mind and soul. I did try to resist, and she tried too, but the tossings and turnings of sleepless nights always communicated themselves to the other partner, so that we ended up in an intensely sensual rhythm, moving together in each other's embrace, then the night clothes would come off and would remain off for the entirety of the musical performance and afterwards.

In the morning I would probe the depths of her regret and it would be real, but at the same time she was a practical woman and understood that people are people, that the flesh is weak. I say that she was practical, yet she could be deeply eccentric too. She would invent theories of her own, about all sorts of things, and believe them with utter conviction.

She told me that walking makes you shorter by eroding your length and that short people were once tall people who had walked too far. It wasn't a joke, she was serious, and that was one of her more sensible ideas. She thought that my refusal to eat meat was a sign of depravity. "Flesh makes you strong!" she would insist, thus I would remind her: "The flesh is weak, Marguerite, you said so earlier."

"True, very true, thank God."

She would laugh and when she laughed her perfect teeth would make me feel ashamed of my own crooked ones. Sometimes she allowed me to prepare salads for both of us. She wanted us to fly to Cameroon together, so she could introduce me to her mother. "She isn't fussy," she said, and this unintentional insult amused me. But her past was a mystery, she tried to explain her previous life but I couldn't follow all the digressions to any meaningful picture, and I didn't even know she had children until one day they came to visit us, three of them, very young and unaccompanied. The doorbell rang and there they suddenly were.

"Aren't you with an adult?" I asked them, but they didn't answer me. French was their preferred language, and they came inside and sat down on the sofa side by side, the smallest one in the middle, while Marguerite appeared from the kitchen with a tray of drinks and food. And they drank and ate and spoke only a few disjointed words and I felt like an awkward intrusion, the same way a curtain that billows too much when a window is left open must feel. It is there in the room, nothing is hurting anyone, but people ignore it with a studied vehemence.

Then the meal was over and the three children stood up and went out the way they had come in, well behaved and precise, and the performance was bizarre to my way of thinking, so I asked her, "Marguerite, my dear, I am astonished that you have children and that they are allowed to walk the streets on their own," and to this she answered, "They don't just walk streets but venture to the airport and back too, for at the moment they live in France with my former

70

partner and come to visit me once a year in the summer and it's summer now, isn't it?"

"Yes, it is, dear," I said, and then I added, "Was one of the three not a child? That's the only feasible explanation."

She nodded. "The middle one, the smallest one, is a man, not a boy. In fact he is my former partner. He was big and tall, strong too, and walking was his passion. He walked everywhere. But he walked too much and just as I warned you, he wore his height away. Now he's short and shrinking a few centimetres every year and soon there will be nothing left but a speck and I pray the children will be old enough by then to care for themselves, because no speck ever made a good father."

Nadine

"BE CAREFUL what you wish for!" That's the famous saying and it's good advice, and I remembered it as I was walking with Nadine along the waterways of Al Khiran, the main pleasure resort of the desert nation of Kuwait, when something that glittered caught our attention in the water. We went over to it and saw an opaque green glass bottle and she picked it up and shook it and it rattled dryly inside.

"A genie?" I asked, because that's what I was expecting and I wasn't surprised at all when she nodded in the affirmative. I would have been far

71

more astonished if the bottle had contained wine, because in this country alcohol is outlawed more strictly than in almost any other land that forbids it. Wine here is much rarer than magic.

"Yes, but he is desiccated and needs fresh water to be activated. Even if the cork had come out it wouldn't have done him any good, because salt water won't hydrate a genie." Nadine dangled the bottle between the thumb and index finger of one hand, as if she didn't care to grip it hard. "I had a friend who found a bottle like this," she explained, "and it broke and cut her hand and her blood brought the genie to life and he was a bad one. I intend to avoid that risk."

But I was baffled and pointed out that blood was more like salt water than it was like fresh, but Nadine shook her head. "Bad genies take liberties," she said, and that was all I could get out of her on the subject. Now I was reluctant to pull the cork and she saw my reluctance and this gave her the urge to draw it on my behalf, which is what she did, then she poured water from her canteen into the bottle, passed it to me and smiled, "Whisper any wish into the neck."

But my wish was that the saying "Be careful what you wish for" wasn't true and that we didn't have to be careful about what we wished for. Yes, that was my wish. Put that in your lamp, genie, and smoke it! But he didn't have a lamp, he lived in a bottle and as he swelled inside the glass vessel and then poured out of it in a spiral of thick smoke that began to take the form of a gigantic being, I knew he had granted my wish even before he nodded down at me and said:

"Your wish is my command."

Nadine laughed and took my arm and pulled me along the shoreline of one of the many lagoons. "Now we need to look for another bottle with another genie in it. The bottle genies only give one wish each, unlike the more generous lamp genies, and you have used that one up. But we won't have to be careful about what we wish for if we ever do get a second chance to make a wish." That was small consolation, but Nadine more than compensated for the missed opportunity, for she is my truly granted wish. And yet still we walk the shores of the desert.

Giuliana

I SEEM TO HAVE TURNED from a man into a woman. The mirror tells me this every time I look into its depths. The mirror is on the wall of the room in the hotel and it glitters like water, like the water in the street outside, the water that *is* the street, for I am in Venice now, where the quality of light is like nowhere else in any other city in the world. But the mirror still has news for me. I have become female.

It's not that I am still roughly the same person that I was but with the features of a woman. That would be understandable. No, my reflection is a woman who is utterly different

73

from a female version of me. She has a quizzical expression but this expression is formed from the arching of her dark eyebrows plucked to the shape of scimitar blades and the pouting of a full mouth that is naturally carmine.

My own eyebrows are bushy and my mouth is professorially thin. But stranger things happen at sea, and Venice is almost at sea, thus it must be here that those stranger things take place, and this is clearly one of them. I pass the mirror as I move between the bed and the bathroom, the window and my suitcase, and the floorboard creaks. Then I turn and look and yes, my reflection peers out at me, and it's a woman. I can't resist gazing into that mirror and making secret gestures.

And the woman makes the same gestures, which proves she is me, but I have doubts, I always have doubts in new places, and I wonder if there's a simpler explanation. What if the mirror isn't actually a mirror but only an internal window between two rooms? In some of these older buildings that's quite plausible. A woman occupies the room next to mine. She too assumes there is a mirror on the wall. Whenever she looks into it she sees a man gazing back. A regular misunderstanding! It is coincidence that we make the same gestures at the same time.

The creaking of the floorboard is the signal that I am about to pass the mirror and it alerts her and she hurries to the mirror on her side, and when I hear a floorboard creaking it's not really the floorboard in my room but the one in hers and

74

it alerts me in turn, which is how we always reach the mirror that is a window at the same moment, thus preserving the illusion. This explanation is neat and comes as a relief and I can relax now and be more focused on preparing to explore the city, to study the maps and step out of this hotel at last, to wander freely.

But my theory is defunct, desperate, contradicted by the evidence, and I know it because I am not alone in my room. You are with me, we came to Venice together, your scimitar eyebrows already arched, full red mouth in a pout, and whenever you approach that mirror, with the accompanying floorboard's creak, you are greeted by the reflection of a man with bushy eyebrows and a thin mouth, the face of a professor who senses his subject is evolving beyond his competence, who no longer understands angles of reflection or the heartaches of refraction.

Lowri

LOWRI IN TUNE never lowers the tone when she sings alone in the bathroom. Sweet but too loud, her voice lifts the roof wide like the lid of a box and up she rides on a wave of sound high over the sea into the night, brushing the stars with her cheeks and making the galaxies blush.

This is preferable, you must surely agree, to banging her head on the clouds?

Claudetta

I
dig
among
memories
of better times
to locate the gems
that validate the excavation
of lost days and nights but the only
jewel of true value among these baubles
was you and the life force within you while your
spirit and body were sunk in the thick riverbank mud
and you toiled at gunpoint to wrest from the ooze
those diamonds that funded the conflict in
that sad and beautiful land where we
found laughter only in dreams
after exhaustion closed
our eyes like a kind
and gentle
mother
who
a
boy doesn't appreciate until
after she has gone and one day I decided to disobey
exhaustion and refuse to sleep and escape instead with
you slung over my shoulders and so gently did I do
this that you didn't awaken even when I waded
through the raging river waist deep into the perilous
safety of the forest and fast asleep in my arms you
trusted me to find a way across the mountains to the
coast and the new life that awaited us there and
despite the fact we had no money we were rich
because we were a pair of rough diamonds of equal
size with enough love inside us to make a third.

Océane

HOW CAN WE COMMUNICATE with each other on this island without power, I ask myself? The volcano has erupted and there's no electricity for people to use, only the lightning in the boiling cloud that still hangs over the top of the broken mountain, and none of us have the wit or wisdom to harness that, and even though the danger is past I still want to know you are safe on the other shore, while I am safe on this side in my little house and still thinking about you, always missing you.

And you are thinking about me, I am sure of it, and I write letters but there is no way to send them, old fashioned letters on paper and scribbled in ink with the nib of an antique pen I found down the side of a sofa many years ago and never discarded. In frustration I crumple the most recent of my letters into a ball and hurl it out of the window and I amazed when the wind rolls it along the dusty road in your direction, faster and faster, and I watch it vanish rapidly into the distance. Can it be possible the wind will deliver it for me?

I daren't hope too much, but this morning the wind changed direction, as fickle tropical breezes love to do, and dressed in its best odours of rum and banana and destruction it bore with it a paper aeroplane that flew into my house through the open window and landed on my desk.

I unfolded it and it was a reply from you, and so we now have a system for exchanging news and advice. But the truth is that our letters are filled with kisses and little else and we learn only what we knew. Don't shoot the messenger, they say, and yet... The volcano still rumbles like distant artillery in a war, like a big gun taking pot shots at the wind, our messenger.

Jessica

JESSICA WAS FROM CHILE and I kept laughing at the shape of her country, a very long and very thin place to come from, and half seriously I asked her what would happen if a person living there grew so fat that their stomach crossed the border without a passport.

Would it be arrested? But she was disinclined to answer this political question and she told me that it wasn't such a thin country after all, that there were many much thinner, that it was only a case of proportion, that Chile was very long in comparison with its width, but that a country such as Andorra, Monaco or San Marino could easily fit within the narrowest part of Chile with lots of space on either side but nobody talks about the thinness of those places, and Jessica felt aggrieved by this and thought it was unfair, that it was picking on Chile, and so to cheer her up, I searched through an atlas to find the nation with the greatest width in relation to its height, and that's how I found Gambia.

Gambia is like a severely truncated Chile that has been rotated exactly 90° from the vertical to the horizontal. In other words, Chile is like part of a longitude line that has put on weight, that has swollen because of some illness, dropsy perhaps, and Gambia is like part of a latitude line with the same problem. Both countries need rest.

And medicine, they also need medicine, but what kind? I'm no doctor and I hesitate to give advice on medical matters, even when those matters are absurd. Suddenly I knew that every country in the world is actually a diseased longitude or latitude line, much more distorted by sickness than Gambia and Chile, which still are recognisable in outline as a parallel and meridian, and that this accounts for all the bad things that happen. A sick land will infect its people. But this implies that healthy countries are only as wide as lines of the most extreme thinness, that they are intangible and infinitesimal, that their cultures and cities, cafés and windmills, anthems, arguments, myths, mosaics, parks and ponds, mopeds and mistakes, rains and shadows, hotels, smiles, spices, shores, abandoned houses with rooms empty as unread books, are all contained within a territory much thinner than a human hair, a glossy black strand.

I hold Jessica around her waist, and she holds me around my waist, to feel if there is any thickness there at all…

Danique

IT BEGAN RAINING very heavily and I didn't have an umbrella with me and my coat was thin and wouldn't keep me dry, but to be honest it's the sensation of a wet head that I really don't like. I can endure rainfall on the rest of my body, I just can't bear it on my face and in my hair, so the obvious solution is for me to wear a waterproof cap, but I didn't have one of those either. I had gone out expecting dry weather because I am an optimist and a fool and then the heavens had opened. We say that the heavens 'open' when it rains but it never looks that way. In fact they look even more tightly shut than before, blacker, more impenetrable, bulging.

Like a suitcase into which too many clothes have been packed, that's how the sky was right at that moment, but I lowered my face and stopped looking at it, because it was lashing my curiosity with thick drops of liquid chastisement. Into both pockets I thrust my hands, to keep those dry at least, and I discovered a plastic bag in the left one, so I extracted it and wore it as a hat. Why not? One does what one can and must. It made a sort of large bonnet as it caught the wind and inflated and I was compelled to push it down on my head with both hands.

I wasn't able to walk along the streets to my house. Too many people were out and about, most of them strolling happily and smugly beneath umbrellas, and every time I neared them,

I had to snatch the bag off and expose my hair and face to the deluge to avoid looking insane or childish and this defeated the point of my improvised hat, so I took a longer but quieter route home down the lanes behind the buildings, a maze of narrow ways that people rarely venture into.

I had discovered this secret world the morning I split my trousers doing exercises in the park. The lanes allowed me to reach the sanctuary of my abode without being laughed at too much for my inadvertent exposure. And now I employed them to avoid a similar mockery on account of my ludicrous headgear with the supermarket name in big orange letters right across its rustling canopy. The lanes are unpaved and puddles love to accumulate here, but I skipped across them, only occasionally having to wade through the larger ones to reach the other side.

I was approaching a bend when I heard a desperate splashing coming from around the corner and I quickly whipped my bag off and crumpled it unseen in one fist. Then I turned the corner and almost collided with a woman and she too had a clenched fist and I thought at first it was in anger at my unexpected appearance. We muttered some incomprehensible apologies and passed each other and walked on, but then I stopped and retraced my steps and found that she was doing the same thing, coming towards me, a grin on her face that matched the one on mine.

And we both were now proud of our plastic bag hats that were full of the future.

Bhagya

BECAUSE I LOVED TEA so much I was far too impatient to wait for the kettle to boil and I needed to find a quicker way of preparing it. Then I had the bright but unusual idea of emptying boxes of tea bags into the hot water tank, which is precisely what I did. At last I had tea all around me, in the network of water pipes that acted like the veins and arteries of the house. I only had to open the hot water tap to obtain instant hot tea and this was a very fine thing, in my humble opinion.

But not in hers. She hated what I had done, she told me that tea should be treated with respect, that where she came from it would be considered sacrilege to rush the making of tea, that the taste of tea that has come out of a tap above a sink was really quite horrible, that I obviously needed to be taught a lesson and that she was the one to teach me. While she was in the middle of telling me all this, I went over to the tap and filled my cup to the brim and drank it with contentment.

Later that day, her voice floated down the stairs, "Bath time!" and this was a surprise, because I normally have a shower and she knows it, so I drained my fortieth cup of tea, and enticed by the sweetness of her tone I went up to see what was transpiring. The bath was full indeed and full of tea. She pointed at it, "Get in!" and now her tone had changed and was so forceful that I daren't disobey. I disrobed instead and lowered myself into the brew and sat there like a mutant spoon.

"Sugar," she said, and I misunderstood and replied, "Honey?" but she wasn't addressing me with a term of endearment, it was a question and I found myself nodding, even though I never take sugar in my tea. Around me curled the steam and a fear of giant lips appearing at the window with the intention of sipping me caused me to tremble and to radiate ripples of strongly flavoured anxiety to the walls of the bath, where they lapped like tongues that drink themselves in futile thirst.

She went away and returned one minute later not with a bag or even a sack of sugar but an enormous sugar cube, I can't imagine where she had obtained it from, and lifting it above her head with both arms, in the same way that our ancestors threw boulders at long extinct tigers, she cast this perfectly regular block into the tea depths. It landed with a massive splash and tea erupted over the walls and ceiling. Then she took hold of me and stirred me in circles until the cube dissolved.

Thank you, dear Bhagya, for curing me of my addiction to tea. Now I only drink coffee, prepared with infinite care.

Kwame

YOU DO NOTHING on the island. That's what you said and then you issued a challenge for me to do less, but how can I do less than nothing? You rock in a hammock all day, so I lay directly under you in the pendulum of your shade, eyes closed and ears stuffed with the sounds of surf until it is time for you to dismount and walk away.

You hips swing in sunset light, your bare feet make an impression that can be followed, so I crawl and slide on the sand like a snake dreaming of legs, because I must do less than you. But do snakes do less than women? You reach the beach bar and enter it and order a cocktail and sip it quietly when it is delivered into your hands.

For you are elegant as well as beautiful and now I don't believe that it is possible to do nothing, because you are everything, you are everything in this world, to the bartender and all who watch you, to me, to the sand, the waves, the rustling trees, to the line of the horizon and the bloated sun setting through it like a comical fruit.

And if it's impossible to do nothing, how might one even begin to do less than nothing? Everything is something. If I sit near you on a bamboo chair without drinking a drop, I am still breathing, sweating, dreaming, I am still a man inspired by you, Kwame, and the inspiration will never end while you exist, so I've failed the test.

But it was never a serious challenge, merely a jest. I walk away, to the sea, looking back at you. The falling coconuts sound like sleepy applause. I am satisfied. Grains of sand glitter on your skin and some coruscate like tiny opals, and night comes and bathes you, but I feel the warmth of your sunshine smile across the entire beach.

Nadja

NADJA WAS A WRITER OF BOOKS and when I asked her who her favourite author was, she looked at me with a strange and impish smile and said, "There is an easy test to work out the answer to your question."

"What is the test?"

"Are you a writer too?"

"I dabble and I have yearnings."

"Yearnings without earnings? Well, that is sufficient. I now want you to imagine a truly gigantic hotel in which every writer who has ever lived is a guest, every writer from the first written word on the first page to the last. At midnight a fire breaks out and quickly becomes a raging inferno. If your first impulse is to escape and preserve your life, then it is assured that your favourite writer is yourself."

"I would call the fire brigade," I muttered.

"Some firemen must be writers. Those that are will already be present in this fictional hotel. They will be able to tackle the blaze without having to travel to the site in a fire engine."

"Is that a good thing?"

Nadja shrugged. We write in the same big notebook. I write from left to right and she writes from right to left. My first page is her last page and vice versa. One day we will meet in the middle and what will happen next is unknown to either of us. Maybe we will stop. Or our words might mesh and continue into each other, snagging on the projecting letters like brave explorers pushing deeper into the thorns of thickets, growths that turn out to be those of culture, not wilderness.

This endless hotel wears holes in my shoes as I tramp the corridors in search of the manager to ask for fresh towels, new soap, extra pillows for the bed, for highly favourable reviews.

Dusica

IT IS EASY TO BE NICE in Nice, but to be even nicer in Niš is the speciality of Dusica, who I went to visit one winter, catching the night train south from Belgrade in the company of a fellow passenger who hung a bottle of beer in a bag out of a window until the water in it froze solid just a few hours later and left a peculiar wine at the top for him to sip. It wasn't especially comfortable, that sleeper train, but it was warm inside, and that makes up for a lot, and my companion was entertaining and not a drunkard, because this was my lucky year, my apotheosis.

The train was travelling to Thessalonica but it reached Niš in the early hours and I disembarked into the snow that compressed underfoot with an agreeable squeaky noise and left my elaborate shoe prints behind like the works of art of a civilization with a love of symmetry and erosion. Then I was embraced by Dusica, who rushed at me from around a corner, for she had woken up early especially to greet me, and I was grateful not to have to roam the empty icy streets for hours before calling for her. She guided me to her apartment and brewed hot tea. I pulled my bulging wallet out of the pocket of my trousers when I sat on her soft sofa, because it was uncomfortable where it was, and threw it down on the floor at my feet.

But then it burst open and fluttered its bank notes everywhere, and for a few magic moments I wondered if they were really butterflies, but no, they settled down again and came to rest on the floor like dead autumn leaves. Dusica said something about the economy, about inflation, and I nodded and we laughed together. I slowly replaced the notes in my wallet and then she said:

"You put them into your wallet with the heads of the depicted historic figures pointing upwards. This is always the case?" And I replied that she was observant, and she added, "I will make a note of it," and that was an excellent joke, but then I felt that my idiosyncrasy called for some sort of explanation and I said, "I worry that if I put them upside down and walk about like

87

that, at least one will be sick and spoil the other notes, because they are faces after all, the faces of people who can't have enjoyed being inverted and stuffed into a giant's pocket."

"The politicians were always in the pocket of someone," Dusica said, but not all the figures on the banknotes were politicians and I still had to fret about those others. She said, "Maybe we are figures on the currency of some mysterious civilization we can't perceive or imagine? Supposing that you and I are just drawings on the banknotes of an alien economy? It would explain any bouts of dizziness or nausea we might experience. On those occasions we've been put into a wallet upside down. It would also explain why we can't always be together."

"Because sometimes we are spent and change hands?"

"We are transacted, my dear."

I gazed up and saw the ceiling of her house loom at me and knew she was right, that we were just figures on banknotes, and that I was one of a lower denomination than her, and that I had been put into a wallet upside down, and I felt chagrin and I felt sick, but Dusica laughed and passed the hot tea to me and yes, it made me feel a little better, a little more soothed and reconciled to my fate as an illustrated piece of paper. We undervalue ourselves often. I wondered what would be bought with me in due course, perhaps a train ticket for a night journey.

Lucy

WE ARE IN BED covered by a thin blanket and holding each other close and the bed begins rocking and heaving, even though we are not moving. The narrow mattress on its wooden frame has become a boat and I wonder if I am dreaming and she wonders the same. We must be sharing the dream in the same way we share almost everything.

The blue carpet in the bedroom is now the ocean and we are adrift in a bed that is a canoe. There is a storm coming, what can we do? Hold onto each other even more tightly, pray to the spirits of the sea to spare us, but are we still asleep or not? This is unclear.

And yet the spirits hear us, they change the shape of our inadequate vessel. The bed expands, becomes a large raft, and now we feel more secure, far from land but grounded, but it keeps growing, it doesn't stop, and the raft turns into an island, an island rippled with ridges that are the creases in the sheets we are tangled up in, and then the bed is no longer an island, it is far too vast for that, but another ocean.

The ridges are waves and they break over our naked bodies that have meshed into one, as if we ourselves are the canoe, but I fear we will turn over, capsize and sink, and yet something happens that makes everything good again.

The sea that is the bed is heaving one way, the sea that is the carpet is heaving another, the result is peace. They cancel each other out, those agitated oceans, and the sum is the serenity we need to maintain us in our safe slumber. One sea riding on a second sea.

The dream, if dream it is, has worked against itself, has tried too hard to disturb us, and its chosen metamorphoses have been deployed in vain, for we are a knot of seaworthy love.

Viviana

THERE I WAS in the pampa and wading through the grass as if there is little else to do in life but be tickled, when she came thundering towards me on her stallion, the bolas whirling around her head. The three balls were like miniature worlds as they caught the sunlight and I was too distracted and stunned to take evasive action. She threw the bolas and it wrapped around my legs and I was immobile, her captive.

I had been told that female gauchos were just as brutal and efficient as their male counterparts and she proved that the gossip was true. First she trussed me up and slung me over her horse and then she rode without any haste in the direction of Buenos Aires, which was a long way from where we were, the south, the region of dagger duels and *yerba mate* drunk from gourds through metal straws. What a jolt!

The weeks passed and we arrived. Buenos Aires reminds me of Paris, one that is more scruffy and neglected, but Paris itself can be scruffy and neglected, so who is to compare and contrast with any certainty? Viviana carried me up many flights of stairs in a tall building and deposited me in an apartment at the very top. This was my home, my prison. I did my best for her, between her strong thighs at night.

She said to me, "Why are you still astonished that I captured you this way and made you mine? What do you think the planets are but the bolas of the sun, who is spinning them round and round in order to cast them at another star, a star he's in love with, a star in the most desirable galaxy of Andromeda. He is waiting for her to come a little closer so he can be sure of his shot. Now love me again, my dear."

Silvia

WE WENT CLIMBING TOGETHER at every available opportunity and when there were no mountains in our vicinity we scaled city buildings or monuments instead, and sometimes walls surrounding palaces, embassies or barracks, and once we broke into a prison and couldn't get out and we had to make a formal appeal to the governor for a pardon, which was granted because he was a climber in his spare time and he understood our compulsion, the craving to proceed in a vertical direction.

At night we climbed over each other, taking it in turns to be the peak, but last spring there was a misunderstanding, a failure in communication, and both of us thought the other was the summit and we were the climber, so we climbed up and up and suddenly realised we were both standing on thin air, that there was nothing substantial supporting our combined mass, and we laughed irresponsibly and tumbled down on the floor. Silvia is one of those people who never lose their temper.

I wish to be more like her. I lost my temper recently and couldn't find it anywhere. I looked in all the obvious places, down the back of the sofa, under the bed, in the pockets of old trousers hanging forlornly on pegs in a wardrobe in the spare room. Then Silvia suggested that maybe I had left it on a ledge on one of our climbs, and this possibility became more likely the more I thought about it, so I decided to return to the location of one of our most hazardous climbs and look there.

It was a statue, an enormous statue on a colossal pedestal, the statue of a celebrated climber, and the ledge in question was his pouting upper lip. Silvia was with me and up we went. It was night but spotlights made it a bright scene. I looked down and realised we were at a higher altitude than we should have been. Silvia said, "The statue itself is climbing," and this was true, it was climbing the beams of the spotlights into the velvet sky, I don't know how or why, taking us with it.

We were like fleas on the body of that statue, going along for the ride, and we had no choice but to accept our situation, so we kept climbing and reached the lip and hauled ourselves over the edge, only to be confronted by a voice that bellowed, "Get away from there!" and I almost fell to my death because the shock caused me to relax my grip, but Silvia caught me and pulled me back and said, "Don't worry, that's not the statue speaking but only your lost temper, which is here!"

And so it was. And I was reunited with it and we sat on the ledge and dangled our legs while the statue kept climbing into the sky until it stood unsteadily but proudly on the top of the very last photon of the last beam of the most powerful floodlight. It was on the summit of its ambition and at the apex of a statue's dreams. Here it sucked in thin air with stone lips that moved like tectonic plates, and I clung tightly to Silvia who is one of those people who never lose their balance.

Ji-su

HOW WILL YOU SAY goodbye to me, Ji-su, when you leave tomorrow? How exactly will you walk out of my life forever? I know you can do it and will do it, we both agree it is the only option open

93

to us, but I am intrigued to learn the method you will use. As I stand in your studio and examine your paintings for the last time, I am happy, not sad, because we have decided to fully accept the facts of our situation and make the most of the little time that remains to us. I am unable to stay, you are unable to accompany me, and this is all that needs to be said, or almost all. I still want to know how it will be, the moment of separation, the moving apart.

"I especially like this one."

"It is a view of the sea from the mountain."

"And this one too."

"A view of the mountain from the sea."

"And what is this one?"

"That is not a painting but the open window. The scene inside the frame is not a painting but the frame of our lives."

"Yes, I thought it was different from the rest."

And we stood very close.

You paint in the traditional style, the style of an earlier century, of your ancestors and the man who designed and constructed the house you live in. The years fell like blossom or like a more original comparison. Back then it was fashionable to represent distance not by use of perspective but by arranging the more distant objects higher up in the picture. Perhaps when you say goodbye tomorrow at the train station you won't move away. You will merely stand above me. You will call for a box or a chair and a porter will provide one and you will climb onto it and will be higher and therefore far from me. While I hold your hand to steady you.

Yasmine

IT WAS ONE OF the oldest continuously occupied settlements in the world, she told me when we arrived, possibly even *the* oldest, and it is true that archaeologists had found evidence of people living there eight thousand years ago, so we walked around it and said hello to those who noticed us, and the sun slowly went down and the peace of an immense world seeped over this landscape too, and I wondered if my ancestors had ever come here and greeted her ancestors.

Unlikely but not beyond the bounds of all reason.

"The weight of continuity is tangible," she said, and I had to agree that yes, it was a peculiarly strange mass to have sitting on the shoulders of one's soul, all those lives with desires and difficulties, heads and hearts, feet and elbows, all congealed together into one enormous lump of past time. Then she added, "Why do you assume that our ancestors were from different places? Yours may have lived here and been neighbours to mine. Everyone is ultimately related..."

"I hope they were good neighbours," I responded.

She shook her head. "If they left here to go elsewhere, as they obviously did, then they didn't get along with my ancestors. They must have been bad neighbours. Or we can compromise and say that both sets of neighbours were at fault. Yet if they had left together it might not have solved the issue. They could have settled down elsewhere and been bad neighbours in a new place."

I said, "Yasmine, I believe that my ancestors were archaeologists. I don't have any evidence for this assertion. I just want to make it anyway." And she laughed and told me that this would complicate matters tremendously, because archaeologists only exist where there is enough accretion of the ancient to make digging for it worthwhile, and if archaeologists had been living in this city when it was founded, that would suggest the city was even older than its own origin.

"Can't something be older than itself?" I wondered.

"Only in terms of feeling," she said.

"Can't an archaeologist live in a brand new town?"

"Yes, but archaeologists are in love with the ancient, so that would be exactly like a lover declining to be with the object of his love. Unless they were only neighbours rather than lovers. Bad neighbours. One had to move and relocate. The archaeologist was the one who moved. And the ancient remained but in truth the ancient can never stay still. It becomes more itself every year."

I nodded and told myself that I fully appreciated her.

And another day passed.

Buivasa

IT WAS ALMOST MY birthday and I was feeling in the mood for sombre jokes because I wanted to spread a little of the solemnity, perhaps to reduce my portion by sharing it out, so I picked up the telephone and called Buivasa and said, "I'm turning forty at midnight, but many years ago when I was a student a fortune teller claimed I would die at the instant of reaching that age. I want to say goodbye now in case it's true."

And I waited for her to be upset.

She replied, "Here in Fiji I am twelve hours ahead of you. As far as I'm concerned you are already forty and therefore you must be dead. Or maybe the fortune teller was wrong." And she laughed.

Her laugh worried me, it meant my joke hadn't worked, that I wasn't as surprising to her as I wanted to be, so in a fit of petulance I said, "The fortune teller was always right," and Buivasa responded without a pause, "Then you are still alive in your own country but dead in this one. Your voice is dead. I must be listening to the voice of a ghost. Yes, it's a ghost that is speaking to me."

I wanted to say, "This is foolish and we should return to sensible talk," and in fact those are the words I tried to utter but for some reason my voice didn't say any of that to her, and instead I heard it say, "I know the secrets of the world beyond this one, the world beyond life. Shall I tell them to you?"

Then I knew that my voice truly was dead even though the body that owned it was still alive, that the reason my poor voice was dead over there was because 'over there' was in a different time zone and existed in the future relative to me, and that because my voice was dead it belonged in the spirit dimension and was now communicating from its eldritch cosmos to our material one.

I wanted to shout, "Buivasa!" but my voice wouldn't let me and it croaked, "Just ask for the secrets and I'll tell them to you..."

Buivasa smiled. I couldn't see her smile but I knew she was smiling because the change in the shape of her mouth altered the tone of her own voice when she said, politely but dismissively, "I have never much cared for secrets. I care for the warmth of the sun and the music of the surf and those are never secrets and never whispered behind anyone's back unless that person chooses to turn it. I am facing the sea right now and about to put the telephone down."

And bless her, that's exactly what Buivasa did.

Raveena

THERE ARE NO RIVERS in Gibraltar, so when she declared that she wanted to take me to a secret river in the territory where two boats were waiting, I was curious and agreed to the proposal. "Why don't we share the same boat?" I asked, and she replied, "They are rather small boats because it is not a large river," and this made sense. "Do you enjoy boat trips?" she pressed and I nodded vigorously and she nodded too and her hair flowed like rapids over the shallows of her face.

I followed her down the street and then off into the undergrowth of an abandoned garden. Space is at a premium in Gibraltar, that tiny peninsula is extremely crowded, but there are still a few undeveloped spots here and there, and on the slopes of the mass of mountain that dominates the locale there is some wild land choked with low bushes. We pushed forward into the scrub and dust and I could see very little but she tightly held my hand until I heard the gentle burbling of water.

The dust settled around us, like a bride disrobing lacy clothes, and we stood on the banks of a river so thin it was like the top of a garden wall. A cat would have rejoiced to walk along its dry bed. But it wasn't dry and in fact the liquid that flowed along it was pure and sparkling and reflected a million sparkles from the sun high above. "The biggest river in Gibraltar, the only

99

one, and it's secret," she said, "and here are your boats." And she indicated two model ships in the trickle.

They were perfect replicas of Spanish galleons from an earlier age and hardly bigger than my shoes. They were prevented from being carried off by the current by a pair of Barbary apes who held slender mooring lines in their mischievous little hands and were clearly waiting for us. Raveena had obviously trained them or maybe they were genuine friends. Before I could clarify this point, she said, "Why delay? These vessels are for your benefit and pleasure," and I understood.

She wasn't coming with me. Would I ever see her again? Doubtful but doubts mean nothing. I slotted my feet into the ships one at a time and yes they were a perfect fit. My stance was that of a skater, one foot behind the other, balancing myself with my arms, and then each ape let go of his line and away I went. It was a quick and drinkable river and I suspected that it originated in a leaking tap high up the slope. And it might carry me to the sea or to a drain, to dismay or to a dream.

Franziska

THE MAN WHO BUYS lingerie for his woman but who always gets the wrong size. This was Franziska's punishment for some unspecified crime, for an outrage committed in a wild dream, and I was the fool without a clue who was the latest agent of her exasperation.

I was hoping the expensive gift of lace and silk in its heart-shaped box would impress and inspire her, such a sweet and fashionable gesture from a citizen who never even ironed his shirts, but the actual effect was closer to the detonation of a large parcel bomb.

"These are far too small! Who do you think I am?"

"I measured you carefully."

"What? How did you measure me? Explain!"

"With my eyes, dearest."

My eyes were defective, they clearly were unable to estimate volume, they were probably only good for ratios. I would have to take them back, secure a refund. And that is what I did in the Viennese autumn with trams clanking their laughter at me, sparking their abrupt corners, as forcefully I pushed and waded through the thick coffee aromas that seeped from cafés like lovely gas warfare, retracing steps.

They were my steps I retraced and my mistake that I made again, for I was persuaded by the shop owner to exchange the gift rather than convert it into money, and I rushed to Franziska with underwear that now was too big and was an even worse insult than before. She said to me, "Take them back but please exchange them properly."

You might not know what she meant, but I did. Yes.

I went in a different direction to a different shop, in a poorer, stranger, morbid part of the city. Oh Franziska! This retail outlet is surely a product of one of your wild dreams, for you have so many, so many wild dreams that they must spill out of your head, and fill up empty spaces in this city of holes, of vacancies in hearts and days.

Just as she wanted, I exchanged them, my eyes this time, for a pair of pale blue orbs that could estimate volumes as well as ratios, but I vowed not to buy lingerie for a woman again, even if I could do so accurately, for it isn't a task meant for me, or for any man.

Jennifer

JENNIFER WAS A BIOLOGIST and one morning over breakfast I said to her, and my curiosity was real, "The Theory of Evolution is everything to you, but surely the theory itself will evolve and change into something different? I can't help but feel this means it runs the risk of eventually evolving into a theory completely unrecognisable to Darwin, maybe even into something diametrically opposed to what it was."

"Yes," she agreed, "but only if it is true. If it false it doesn't endanger itself in that way. It's safe from logic."

How can anything be safe from logic? Jennifer has a smile that causes all the doubts in my life to hurry towards extinction, but they pause on an edge of a cliff and look at me for final confirmation. I nod at them, go on and jump, don't hold back, but then a fog descends and I can't tell if they have obeyed me or are still hesitating.

"If the theory is mistaken it can't change and cancel itself out, thus it remains intact. If the theory is correct it might change into its enemy, its own refutation, but the act of change will prove it was right all along, so how can it lose? If it loses it still wins."

I change the subject. "Fogs descend but a mist arises."

"Frogs?" she questions me keenly.

She has misheard, beautiful Jennifer has, but no, my doubts there on the edge of that cliff are hopping now, and croaking as they plunge down to their doom and yet I fear that as they pile up below, the mound of dead green flesh will cushion those that come later. My recent doubts will have a good chance of surviving, will stand a good chance, stand on legs tense as springs in a season remote from spring.

My hands are upon the table, they hop onto her, she sighs, but what is the meaning of her sigh, I'm not sure. A mist arises. My curiosity always is real, but real things can be false too, in fact they usually are. The theory is robust, it withstands the rub of paradox, just as the table leg withstands the rub of my breakfast leg against it, and conversely my leg declines to succumb to the eroding pressure of the table, but my hands fall away like doubts again and return to the cereal spoon.

Brankica

IN THE CITY THAT is overrun with statues I found myself pushing through the crowds in order to reach my rendezvous in time. Brankica had arranged for us to eat in one of the cafés at the Old Bazaar. I threaded my way up the hill but every street was thick with pedestrians. I had never seen Skopje so busy before, so full to bursting with humanity, and I wondered if today was a national holiday. The flags were flying over the public buildings, true, but they always do that, the sunbursts on each enormous banner shining as if the sun had been replicated there, but on fabric and not by a sculptor, yet these vast symbols gave off no warmth, in fact they cooled as they flapped and my sweat evaporated.

I was late now, the mass of people was so great, and I worried that I would create a bad impression, but Brankica received me gracefully, as she always does, and we sat down at a small table in a narrow courtyard, and I was breathing heavily and she was smiling, and we ordered plates of food from the waiter who was already standing next to us, and then I turned my attention to her, but from the corner of my eye I was aware how slowly the waiter was moving, how stiffly and without energy, like a shadow puppet that has fossilised. But my suspicions weren't sufficiently aroused yet, and when Brankica toasted me with her glass I responded with alacrity and sang her praises.

After twenty minutes, I said, "The food is taking a long time."

"Yes, but that's because of the cook."

"Why is he so slow, Kika?"

"Because he is a statue. It's unfortunate but true."

"I am astonished to hear this."

"The waiter is a statue too. He is mounted on little wheels and the wind is strong enough to move him along, but not very fast. The cook, however, is in the kitchen where there is nothing to hurry him."

"How long must we wait?" I asked hungrily.

And my hunger was not for food, not at all, quite the opposite in fact, for I could scarcely concentrate on filling my mouth when my heart was the starved part of me, the hole that was filling up with her presence, with the echoes of her melodious being, but I still wanted more, wanted second helpings and dessert, the *celufki* of her eyes, the *baklava* of her soul. Then she replied sweetly and oddly:

"Until the wind and the rain and time erode them all."

And that's how I knew the truth.

Skopje is a city overrun with statues. The government had decided to turn it into a theatre of a capital, to make it a light opera in stone, and now there were more statues than dreams, and the flesh people had left, they had moved elsewhere, and the crowds on the streets were no longer real and would never disperse of their own accord, and the only two living people were Brankica and I, but it still seemed a full city, for when the authorities ran out of heroes to reproduce in stone they had ordered statues to be carved of ordinary folk, and all these former inhabitants had been left behind, and even Brankica herself was one of them, petrified in the act of crossing a bridge over a river at the bottom of which the statues of suicides resided.

Mona

A MAN, A PLAN, A CANAL: Panama. We all know that palindrome and we are impressed. It is one of the best ever fabricated. But it is rather one sided, it fails to recognise that women use the canal too, and yes you can assume it's about the construction of the canal, which was mostly or entirely done by men, but that's just an assumption, it really is, because it might equally be about a man sailing on the canal, and his plan doesn't have to be a plan of the waterway, it could be a plan to drink a cocktail when he reaches the other ocean on the far side of the isthmus.

I am that man on that boat and I am making slow but steady progress, but I don't crave a cocktail, that's the last thing I want, I have never been a devotee of alcohol, what I want and need is a woman, not any woman, but her. And she should be with me on this trip, but she isn't, and I'm not sure why or where she went after I boarded the boat. She said she would be a few more minutes, she urged me to cross the gangplank without her, so I did, but she didn't follow me, and we sailed without her and I wasn't in a position to prevent the vessel departing.

A woman, a plan, a canal: Panamowa. That word makes no sense. But when I treat it as an anagram it yields her full name. Mona Wapa. And I am delighted about this, but why should I be delighted? She isn't here to share the triumph. I shout the name over the railings on deck. Mona. And she answers me and says, "I wanted to stretch my legs, that's why I didn't accompany you." It is night but the water glimmers and shimmers and it's not difficult to see her down there. "Legs?" I ask dryly, as dryly as sound allows. I need my element to be reinforced.

"Fins," she agrees and thrashes her tail and I reflect that even though I never knew she was a mermaid until this very moment, I'm not dismayed or censorious, only slightly curious to learn what fee the canal authorities will charge her when we reach the far side, and how she will pay, lacking pockets, how I will pay, lacking a sense of responsibility, how the subject will then be quietly ignored because it is too original, and how we will be together, discharged into the next ocean, but with awkwardness as well as affection between us because she is half fish.

Dagmara

I CAME HOME FROM WORK, weaved my way between the obstacles on the floor, winced as something bit my leg, then I saw that the bedroom door was open. Dagmara sat on the edge of the bed and she smiled winsomely and gestured alluringly and I dropped my briefcase, shrugged myself out of my jacket and went to confront her. "I'm ready, why waste time?" she asked.

She was already in her stockinged feet, so I took my shoes off and climbed onto the bed. I stood there for a moment and waited while she stood too. We both moved as close to the centre of the mattress as possible. And then we grinned at each other, counted one, two, three! And began jumping. Why not? Why delay until bedtime for this most invigorating of rituals? Why wait?

Up and down we went and the springs squeaked and groaned like the donkeys of the Nizina Środkowoeuropejska when they are overloaded with market produce and I feared the springs might break through the mattress or that the bed might collapse or the floor might give way, but fear was part of our delight and we bounced higher and higher, Dagmara and I, like fledgling angels.

Show me a man who has never used a bed as a trampoline and I will show you a man who would never wear a tea cosy on his head even if he were locked in a room with no other object for a day. Such a man is a fool, an abject dullard, a loon. Higher and higher bounced Dagmara and I and we linked arms like jolly comrades instead of undulating lovers. And then disaster struck…

It was inevitable. A man who has never used a bed as a trampoline is not a real man, but he is also a man who does not penetrate the ceiling with his head. Ditto for the woman who is with him. We went straight through the plaster and emerged in the upstairs apartment and we were stuck there, our heads in one domicile but the rest of our bodies in our own. "Help, set us free!"

But the inhabitants of that apartment didn't care about our plight. They ignored us, they were too intent on enjoying themselves, on hastening to their bedroom, so as the man went past I bit him on the leg. It was all I could manage to do. He winced but did nothing else, then he went into his bedroom and I heard laughter as he and his woman began jumping up and down on their mattress.

Now I know why my own leg was covered in bites and what those roughly round and hairy objects that had appeared on our floor were. An apartment block of joyous lovers using their beds as trampolines and getting their heads stuck in their ceilings. I am bored now, there's nothing to do here, I wish someone would put a tea cosy on my head. And Dagmara wishes exactly the same.

Saturnina

LET ME TELL YOU now what Saturnina told me, that the dance known as limbo began as an extended metaphor, the emergence or return to life from oblivion, with the bar set at its lowest point and then gradually raised. This order of procedure was reversed for the sake of showmanship years later.

But she still did it the original way, there in one of the most obscure corners of her island, and yes it has corners because Trinidad is a square, a badly drawn one but nonetheless a four sided geometric shape, whereas she was nearly all curves and had few corners.

And yet I managed to corner her in that bar in Port of Spain and it was sunset and we went out for a walk in the dust and the noise and beyond the chaos there was fire in the sky and coolness in the scented breeze and it seemed that I was yearning to be far away, although the same yearning had brought me here, and now I had Saturnina I knew all yearnings were useless, that I was at my destination at last, that wanderlust forevermore would be just a case of running on the spot. And she promised to dance for me, to show me how to limbo properly.

The following day we went on motorcycle to the far south and she shouted in my ears the directions I had to take, because she was riding pillion behind me and I didn't know where we were going, and we skidded and slithered over the narrow tracks and though we could have taken the coast roads we didn't. There will always be things we can do that we don't. We can eat *tippi tambo* for breakfast, if we like, or we can not, if we prefer. We don't have to justify it. I ducked under low hanging branches and I felt that this was my own perilous limbo dance.

But her version was eventually far more perilous than mine. For when we reached the spot she had in mind, it turned out to be the hubbling bubbling hell of the infamous Pitch Lake at La Brea, the world's largest natural deposit of asphalt, and a sticky sickly torrid mess of a place, though I for one was grateful for the tarmac that comes from it and smoothes my motorcycle jaunts through the streets of Port of Spain, but I asked in a panic, "Honey, why are we here?" and she answered, "Because this is certainly the nearest thing to Limbo I know."

And before I could stop her bewitching me, she dismounted from the saddle and approached the lake, lithe and nimble and mournful with her life a cargo of truths and pains that I would never know in the vessel of her body, and she danced

111

and danced, a dance to return to life from oblivion, from the oblivion of this life, this world, this fate, from present time into some better reality, and the bar was set as low as it could be, lower than the ground, and while it seethed and palpitated, I witnessed Saturnina dance below the lake, completely beneath it.

No part of her form touched the lake that was now above her, she was too skilled, too assured, too perfect for that. Not a ripple radiated from her, she was under the bed of the lake and when she finally emerged on the other side, not a single drop of pitch glistened on her skin like the obsidian face of one of the lake's charred victims, for in previous years people had indeed fallen in. Saturnina was reborn and I never saw her again but often in Port of Spain I pass a bar and I wonder if it's the same one in which I once found heaven in an extended metaphor.

Esther

I WROTE A FAUX five-word poem for her.

It goes like this:

See Esther / take a / siesta

And then I thought deeply about turning it into a faux eight-word poem by simply adding the words: *in the nude.*

But I didn't, because that's rude.

Söökhlö

Blown by the wind	the ship on wheels arrives	outside the forsaken hotel	where I am staying silent	saving my words for her
her hair is scorched and	from the burning plain	leaping off the weary camel	she lands on booted feet	with perfect poise and style
whips the beast onwards	and stops near the temple	she lands in my arms	grinds to dust the objects	cradled there already
the steed of my chariot	each wheel a mandala	trusting me to catch her	and the force is so strong	she listens in a deep trance
pounding like a crazy drum	the vessel stops praying	without risk of dropping	through the planet's crust	my bones play a tune
		because my deep desire		
		To embrace her so tightly		
The city of Elista waits	sheltered in its obscurity	Is greater than gravity or	the attractive force of	Söökhlö the Kalmyk girl
under the sun that blinds me	like a chess player that	momentum or any law that	your thoughts can devise	has utterly confounded
a man in the mirror maze	disguised as a black bishop	Physics may have passed	out of his old memory and	expectations with her words
reflects the tired hours	slides diagonal in the night	in the courts of the cosmos	so frozen is the posture	my clockwork heart stops
and goes back for seconds	an unseen and broken doll	when reality was young	a semblance of precise life	and it waits just as I do

Ophelia

BALDNESS ISN'T NATURAL but a result of civilization. It surely comes from generations of wearing tight hats.

In our original condition, evolution would never choose baldness because the moonlight reflecting off the shiny scalp would give away our position to predators in the jungle. Men with thick heads of hair are less likely to be pounced on by tigers. They are more likely to be used as a paintbrush by gorillas, yes, I'll concede that point, but pounced on by tigers, no.

That's what I said to her as I proudly allowed the wind to ruffle my hair. Then she answered, "Or maybe an improved diet means that modern men grow taller than early people did and rise above the hairline."

"What do you mean?"

"That your ancestors never grew through their own hair. Human height evolves at a faster rate than the elevation of the hairstyle. You haven't managed that feat. You are stuck at a primitive stage of development."

"I think that's unlikely."

"As you are so fond of reminding me, there are more things in heaven and earth than are dreamt of in your philosophy."

"Hamlet said that to Horatio long before I did."

"And was it equally true then?"

"Yes. And the moment Hamlet uttered those

words they were added to Horatio's philosophy. But Horatio's philosophy already existed in the location called 'heaven and earth' because that's where Horatio himself existed, so if we use the letter X to represent 'heaven and earth' it turns out that Hamlet was stating that there are more things in X than are contained in that part of X that understands that there are more things in X than are contained in that part of X that understands that there are more things in X... and so on forever and ever!"

"And we simply don't have sufficient time, do we?"

"No, we certainly don't."

She reached out and tangled her fingers in my hair and then she pulled, hard, but nothing came off. I wasn't wearing a wig.

"It really is natural? In that case..." and she whistled.

A lumbering form came through the undergrowth. My voice was a little nervous as I said, "There are no gorillas here."

"Not in the wild, but we have zoos, you know."

Sreyneang

THE RUINED TEMPLES are overgrown and even more beautiful to my eyes as a result but this is entirely my own perspective and I wonder how I might feel when I am decayed and my ribcage filled with orchids and other jungle flowers and the people who come along prod me with a foot and say, "He's more lovely and mysterious in this condition and will look much better in photographs."

Time passes and objects soften and crumble but that's not all they do. Sometimes they acquire a melancholy or serenity they never originally had. Then we judge them for those qualities. And in our minds, as we reverse the years and restore the objects to their pristine condition, we forget to erase what has been added later. The skeleton regrows its flesh but keeps the orchid heart.

She climbs over the broken statues and finally sits on the head of one so rounded and eroded that it's impossible to tell what god it was. She dangles her legs above me and I feel the tugging in my chest, a fluttering of the flower petals, an urge not to join her up there but to leap and snatch one of her sandals from her feet, to run off with it into the green paradise that is all around us.

That paradise would rapidly turn into a hell if I did that. Wandering lost, doomed, delirious, my bones aching to throw off the flesh that stifles them, I would sit down under a tree and begin to accumulate the mystery that future explorers will praise. So I restrain myself and simply stand there, but now I have the desire to pull her legs like ropes in a belfry, alternately, to ring her soul.

"It is time to go," I say.

She shakes her head at this and replies, "We

are beyond that now, far beyond. It is time to stay. Why are you anxious?"

"I have a flower instead of a heart, that's why."

"No, it is a butterfly..."

I shrug because her words don't make me feel better. I understand that I have died and been dead a long time, that some future observer has rewound me in their mind to see what I am like in my own age. And here I am again, but I have brought along with me the things that the centuries have given me. I am essentially unknowable and yet I evoke an unspecific nostalgia. And I call out.

She slips off her perch, off the time-melted head of the god, and she soars with the erratic and delightful flight pattern of the butterfly and then at last she swoops at me and enters through my chest and folds her wings where my heart should be. And so I sink to the ground inconclusively and wait for it to stop being the time to stay and for it to start being the time to go again. One day.

Stella

IT IS GOOD TO SLEEP under the stars. But there are conditions. It isn't always safe without careful consideration of the factors involved. On an iceberg one may easily freeze to death under the stars. One may mix one's bones with those of

117

camels' under the stars in a waterless desert. The stars don't care and will do nothing to help. There they are, shining for themselves, and all the romance is our decision alone.

They don't even shine for the benefit of navigators, so why should we expect them to favour our love affairs? Stella and I slept under them on a beach that is our favourite beach. The sand is soft but it was still an astute move to pat it flat at the designated spot. Ridges and bumps are like slow motion chops and punches in the middle of our dreams. We unrolled two sleeping bags and suddenly our bedroom was the world. Ships out at sea blazed their own lights in tighter constellations than those above and the moon was thin and low, almost theoretic.

Stella said, because she always says something philosophic before we go to bed, "If we are sleeping *under* the stars, then they must be sleeping *on* us," and I answered, "The stars don't sleep at night but during the day when we are awake," and this reply seemed definitive but my confidence turned out to be misplaced, like the electric torch I thought I had brought along but couldn't find anywhere, because Stella countered with, "We are awake right now and it is night, so there must be some overlap, and a few of those stars at least are probably sleeping."

I looked up and was compelled to agree that many of them did seem a little drowsy, if not fully somnolent, especially those directly overhead. I then asked the fateful question, "So what are the implications?" and Stella scented victory and whispered, "We are ridges and bumps and if they are sleeping on us they will try to smooth us out."

"Just as we do with the beach and other surfaces," I said and I sighed because my comfortable night was over, and until dawn I felt the pressure of the starlight over my entire body as it attempted to gently flatten me like a patch of lumpy sand, and when dawn came I was a gingerbread man or petrified shadow and I shrugged off my sleeping bag and hobbled on my awkward legs down to the shoreline where I embraced Stella with my vast flat ungainly arms in the sunrise surf.

Amira

THERE WAS A SALSA COMPETITION announced in the newspaper. I saw it and called Amira on the telephone and told her all about it. We danced salsa, Amira and I, and we were both in need of money. It seemed that we could prepare for the event and maybe even win the prize. We stood a chance, a good chance, and it was worth a try in the same way that praying is worth a try, that remaining alive is worth a try.

We arranged to meet as often as we could and practice. In the light of dawn we would dance on the beach, in the car park at lunchtimes, behind the library after work, late at night under the moon or in the rain, and in her narrow bedroom, perfecting the moves, the footwork, the turns, every flourish that is regarded as fine styling. We became the dance and salsa became us. We embodied it in our flesh.

I cut out the advert for the event and pinned it to my wall despite the fact it was nothing special, had no illustrations or exclamation marks or big letters, was just a plain notice to the effect that the competition would be held in the town hall the following month and that anyone could apply to enter by turning up on the day. We practiced every spare minute of our busy lives until we became a real couple.

My sincere belief was that we were now likely to come first, but at the same time I didn't want to run the risk of being too confident, and yet the joy of the dance was one with our bones. We went to the town hall at the designated hour, breathing deeply and rhythmically to calm ourselves and then nodding to each other before passing through the door. And there on the threshold we were given the utensils.

Utensils? What equipment is required for salsa apart from momentum and feet? The attendants gave us a chopping board, a cleaver, tomatoes, a big white onion each, bunches of herbs. We cradled these in confusion as we entered the hall and emerged into the smoke of a makeshift canteen, a temporary kitchen filled with the hiss of gas stoves and no other music. It had been pointless, our striving, our hope.

We exchanged glances and smiled with difficulty and set down on the floor what we held in our arms and took each other in those arms because this was not our kind of salsa, our kind was different. And despite the fact the pulsation of the chopping around us wasn't quite right, we danced out of the hall to that music, completing a full circuit, then passing the gaping attendants without stepping on their toes.

We proceeded down the street like that, dancing, oblivious of anyone who might be watching, and the olive oil that sizzled in saucepans in the hall behind us might as well have been under the soles of our shoes now, so smoothly and slickly did we move, and though we remained poor and hungry it didn't seem to matter until the song ended but that would never occur, because we were the musical notes.

Catarina

SHE WAS A CAT in a former life, this was obvious, and when it rained I had to laugh at her alarmed expression. She enjoyed being stroked and sitting on shelves. She often slept curled up on my lap. But one day when I made a joke about her feline nature she said:

"You forget that a cat has nine lives. I'm only the reincarnation of one lost life of one cat. The other eight lives have become other people who could be anybody or anywhere. And you might even be one of them. This means our relationship is narcissistic."

"The chances of that being true are less than—"

"Seven hundred and seventy-seven million to one," she purred, and I was so startled by the precision of her calculation that I didn't ask her to explain it. I just chuckled as one does at a story that isn't really funny. I thought about the entire population of the earth, as it was back then, and divided it by the number of a cat's lives.

"There are eight others alive who were once you. I can accept that. If I am one of them, however, I don't see what we can do. Do you think that relationship counselling might be useful?"

"No, but we can go to the fair tomorrow instead."

I didn't press her for more details. I just continued to stroke her head and the following day we went to the fair, but she insisted that I carry the large wardrobe mirror with me under one arm. I had spent an hour with a screwdriver removing the mirror from that item of furniture. I didn't ask questions, I just did her bidding, she was a cat and I was a man and when one is a man, at least the right sort of man, one rarely disobeys a cat. We paused outside the Tunnel of Love where she said, "Now you must take a boat but go with the mirror as your lover."

I understood. This was a test. The perfect narcissist is in love with his own reflection as well as his own imagined qualities. And so I drifted into the mouth of the Tunnel with the mirror on the seat beside me and when I emerged at the exit I saw that Catarina had vanished. There was no point calling for her. She had gone behind the mirror, looking in the logical but wrong place for the original of the reflection, and now she would always be behind it, the mirror a barrier between us.

Or perhaps it was me who had gone behind the mirror during the trip through the Tunnel. That would be a more plausible explanation for what happened that day. I am one of the other lives of the cat, so when the boat emerged it contained only the mirror, and Catarina waiting for it wouldn't be astonished that I was always behind it and effectively gone. Nor would the owner of the ride notice anything amiss. He would see himself sitting in the boat in the mirror and pull a long face.

Emily

"I KNOW DIDDLY SQUAT," she said, and at first I thought she was being modest, but she really did know him personally, that incredible musician who played a guitar behind an inscrutable radiance that was composed of the sounds he created, and she, Emily, an accomplished musician herself, promised to introduce me to him that very night after the show. But first we had to find the show. Diddly Squat keeps the venues of his gigs secret, it's one of his affectations, and the only way you can find him is by following your ears through the backstreets.

New Orleans is everything that people say it is, more than what they write about, remember for decades afterwards, with their inner nostrils as well as their inner eyes, because the aromas are what stick in the mind, the very unhealthy fried foods that can be spicy as love, as greasy as death, as fattening as the act of giving up. Emily pulled me by the arm and we ran up and down every alley and the rain had stopped but large raindrops that were fatter than pearls hung on the iron balconies above us and usually fell with the vibration from the trombones.

For yes, there was street music and this confused our sense of direction, because it was harder to hear the picked strings of a gently amplified guitar amid the brassy jazz and glissando pomp, and in fact the whole act was one of pure chance, but chance did what it should, and that's how we ended up exhausted outside a shady dive, breathing fast and shallow, as shallow as the dive itself, and the shallowest of dives is the belly flop and bellies were flopping inside for sure when we took a peek through what was a front door though it looked like a coffin lid.

And Emily said, "This is it, we are here, we stopped for a rest after running and it just happens that Diddly is inside."

So we straightened up and leaned on each

other as we pushed that lid open and ambled our skeletons inside. And there was Diddly on an awkward stool and he was dimmed by the mists of minims his fingers threw up from the strings and he caught sight of Emily and winked. A murmur ran through the entire audience at this, for Diddly never altered his expression, no how, no way, for anyone, a thing unheard of, and suddenly I wondered.

What did I really know about Emily, about her past, present and future, about the circles she moved in, the squares she sat in, the triangles she became entangled in, the polygons that were like expensive rented office spaces of the heart and soul to her? I knew little, less than little, nothing at all, in fact I knew Diddly Squat.

And then as if by some magic he winked at me too. Because I knew him, I knew Diddly Squat, and I hugged Emily and everything was resolved, not only the chords but the feelings that were slightly between us like a wedge of notes.

Princessa

SHE WANTED TO BE TREATED like a princess, so that's what I did, in keeping not only with her wish but also her name, which was too good to waste by arguing with her. I went and bought some peas and put one of them under her mattress when she wasn't there.

It was a dried pea, very hard, that wouldn't be squashed flat, and when it was bedtime I waited in my own bed for her reaction.

The remaining peas I had soaked in a saucepan and boiled when they were soft enough and I had turned them into a reasonable soup that could be slurped by anyone with lips, not only royal people. We shared it.

And now I was in my own bed listening to her as she lay in her bed and I thought: If she is a real princess, then she must feel the pea through the mattress thickness, despite the powerful springs and stuffing, and the discomfort of having such a legume with all its persistence and tightly packed obliviousness directly under her spine will prompt her to thrash about in bed and in the morning she will be exhausted from her ordeal, because this is the traditional test.

If she sleeps soundly, then she isn't a princess after all, and it will be much harder for her to convince me that she ought to be treated like one. Let's see what happens.

It is never so straightforward, however, and in the morning when she awoke and rose as refreshed as ever, I had my doubts. Perhaps there were different grades of princess, an entire order of them less sensitive, tactile, delicate, than the others. A set of tough and rugged princesses. One pea over the span of just one night wasn't enough to confirm or disprove anything.

I needed to add more. And that's what I did. I went out and bought more dried peas and didn't turn these into soup but secretly positioned them, one more every day, under her mattress, until there were at least a hundred peas beneath her, and yet she still didn't seem to feel any pain or irritation, and finally I had to conclude, at the end of the experiment that had lasted the entire summer, that she absolutely wasn't a princess, not in any meaningful sense of the word, that she was just herself.

Then it occurred to me, though it was a belated and frustrating insight, that more peas would exert less pressure on the underside of the mattress than one would, and that I had been gradually weakening the ordeal rather than amplifying it, because the force generated by her mass was now spread out equally on all the peas. It's the same principle that allows a fakir to sleep on a bed of many nails but not on a single spike. I had forgotten all this and failed as a result.

I opened my heart and mouth to her, confessing everything, and she invited me to jump into her bed, but as I did so she leapt out of it. My trajectory was tangential and when I landed on her mattress it rolled off the frame of the bed, the round peas acting like ball bearings.

Her bedroom door was open and the mattress sailed through it and bumped down the stairs, a raft with me as a passenger, and slid through the front door into the street, which happened to be a hill. Momentum was responsible for everything that happened next.

I remained on the mattress, too nervous to

abandon it at such a dangerous velocity, and so I accelerated down the slope and reached the bank of the river, which is more like a ravine than an ordinary bank, and over the edge I went, tossing and turning as I did so, even though I wasn't seeking a more comfortable position, and when I hit the water I soon learned how to rest in peace as well as rest on peas.

Jane

THE SUNFLOWER in Jane's garden was an unusual one. It was planted in the exact centre of her largest flowerbed and it consisted of an enormous bloom on a long stalk.

When she went out in the early morning to drink her coffee on a bamboo chair, the stalk would be drooping to the east, the bloom touching the ground, and slowly the stalk would straighten itself, pulling into the sky the flower, which would change colour from red to orange to yellow. At noon the bloom would tower high above her and she could bathe in its shadow, which was surprisingly warm on the skin.

As the afternoon progressed, the stalk would begin to sag again, but this time the droop would be towards the west. The huge flower would ripen in colour, darkening, softening, turning a deep russet before touching the ground, where it would come to rest, as if sleeping. But what happened after that, Jane couldn't guess.

128

Night in the garden was still a mystery to her. By the time the stars came out, if that's what they did, she would be curled in her hammock and fast asleep. In her dreams, there was no answer to the question. It was always a forbidden secret.

Eventually the mystery was solved. As she basked in the midday shadow of the mighty bloom, a butterfly flitted past her head and then flew up and came to rest on the surface of the flower. Other butterflies joined it.

Bees too. Within minutes the entire area of the yellow flower was covered by a mixture of the two kinds of insects and the result was an unintentional eclipse. The differing bodies of the butterflies and bees were like the seas and highlands of the moon.

Jane felt a chill and the birds went silent. Then to her astonishment the stars appeared. They were tiny sunflowers and there were thousands of them. They sprinkled the garden like constellations. Jane was enthralled but knew that eclipses don't last long.

She began walking towards one of the tiny flowers but it was much further away than it seemed. It was just an illusion that it was in her garden. The reality was that it was beyond her property. She kept walking, forsaking her home, but it remained tiny. She realised at last that the stars were giant sunflowers too but at vast distances. And now she is lost in the immense spaces between gardens.

Sandy

Why do you want an hourglass shape so badly, I asked her
but she merely shrugged and tightened the straps of her
corset until her cheeks were flushed and her breath
came in shallow gasps like a woman who is
riding a roller coaster at the fair and has
just reached the apex of the curve
on the way up and is about to
begin the plunge on the
far side, and that was
the only answer
she cared to
give me,
my girl
with
the fair
hair of red
and gold, but
days passed and
I saw that she was
losing that hair, that it
was growing shorter and
retracting into her skull and
that her feet were becoming hairy
instead, as if compensating for the loss
above, and then I understood what being an
hourglass means when you have hair the colour of
a faraway beach and the sands of time pass through you.

Joramae

IT'S TRUE THAT MY HOUSE was dirty, an awful mess, I hadn't cleaned or tidied it for years, but I didn't really want her interfering with the way things were. I had equipment in my study that was fragile, delicately balanced, it couldn't be moved or even nudged. I told her this but she remained unhappy. In the end she insisted that she be allowed to clean for me and I reluctantly agreed but I was aware it was unfair on us both, unfair on her to do the chores I should be doing for myself, and unfair on me for my wishes to be disregarded. So I went out for a walk.

While I was gone she began the task of cleaning everything. She found items that I had lost and forgotten about, including my large red umbrella, the one big enough to shelter two or three people easily. She scrubbed the grime off every surface in all the rooms, using muscle power mainly, but also bicarbonate of soda and vinegar, which fizzed like the froth of an enraged mouth. But my mouth wasn't enraged now. During my walk I calmed down. I decided to go to the shop to buy a large box of chocolates for her, as a gift and a way of saying thanks.

She had promised not to touch the equipment in my study but only to clean all the other rooms. I strolled down the streets, heard what sounded like thunder beyond the town but felt no rain on my shoulders, found the shop and went in. When I came back out with my prize I decided to give it a tour of the town before returning home. I had no desire to stand over her like an overseer while she worked. Much better to take the chocolates for a walk through all the bustle and life of the afternoon and then present them to her as she wiped the last windowsill.

The shadows slowly lengthened until eventually I was home again. Thunder still was rumbling and now it was a continuous roar but without any rain. I stood in front of my house and she was there, almost exactly as I had imagined, polishing the front door knob, and she declared, "It's all done." Then she went inside and I was about to follow her when a deafening crash assaulted my ears and my vision was obscured by dust. The ground shook and I was thrown to my knees. When I looked up, the clouds of dust had dispersed and my house was gone.

The earthquake was very brief but hugely destructive. She stood in the middle of the rubble, holding the umbrella above her, and then I noted how clean every part of the destroyed house was, how shiny and pleasing to my eye, all the fragments, blocks and crumbs of the place I had called home, and I asked, "You didn't attempt to clean my seismograph, did you?" and from her expression I knew she had dusted it at least and I stepped forward and gave her the chocolates and as we stood together under the open umbrella it finally began to pour with rain.

Yousra

A JOURNEY of a thousand miles begins with a single step, but when you are a millipede a single step is already a journey of a thousand feet. Yousra is an athlete and she runs so fast that her afterimage makes her look like she has many legs, that she is an elongated version of herself, a millipede that shall never be caught by whatever it is that chases her. I chased her on my bicycle once but she outran me easily.

I wonder at the persistence of her afterimage. Nobody has ever had an afterimage like Yousra's. It remains for hours, days, weeks, fading slowly like lacquer, and it is hard, solid, three-dimensional. It lingers not only on the retina but in reality too. One can approach it at an angle in a hurry and bounce off it with an expression of astonishment. If Yousra ran in a circle around a man she would imprison him.

Unless that man is a champion jumper, he would be fenced in until the afterimage dispersed like a crumbling wall. I practice leaping high, I lope and fling myself over bars, for I can also be an athlete and achieve a great feat, but in a different direction. One day I will be able to spring over that afterimage that has formed a labyrinth around me. Until then I will do the expected thing and explore it carefully.

The maze is a complex one and I am soon lost. The most traditional of situations for a man like myself, to be lost in a relationship. Yousra made the maze when I was sitting on my chair outside, doing the crossword in a newspaper, not paying attention to anything around me. Now I am paying the price. It will fade eventually, certainly before I learn to jump over it. I will keep probing deeper into the tangle.

I know that a Minotaur awaits me at the very centre, but I don't know what kind of Minotaur it will be. Maybe a very docile one. Ultimately she is an extremely kind woman and not prone to encouraging nasty monsters to take up residence in her afterimage patterns. Much later, but I can't say when, we will be reunited, and in bed we will thrash in the act of love and her afterimage will be more like a spider.

Hilola

THE FULL MOON was rising over the city and it just so happened that I was walking along a street that is very straight and also deserted and buildings and traffic didn't compromise my view of the wonderful spectacle. And I wondered, as I always do in these circumstances, why the moon seems so much bigger close to the horizon and so much smaller after it has climbed a little distance into the sky. Because it is, after all, the same moon and it logically ought to retain the same dimensions. When I returned home, my thought was one that I voiced to Hilola.

134

She said, "There are many plausible explanations. It could be that the air acts as a magnifying lens, because when the moon is rising the light it shines passes at an angle through the atmosphere to reach an eye. There is subsequently a lot more air in the way."

"Interesting. But give me another explanation."

"Well, perhaps it is merely an optical illusion. When it's low it is near objects on the ground and we are better able to compare it with them. We see a hill on the horizon and the moon looms behind it, so we assume it is larger than the hill but also here on the ground. Then as it continues rising it becomes isolated and seems to shrink."

I shrugged and didn't ask for more theories. I was sleepy and decided to have an early bedtime. But something woke me after less than an hour, an eerie sensation, and I opened my eyes.

Hilola's face was rising over the foot of the bed and it was enormous, smiling, radiant, wise beyond her years, but also slightly sinister, Despite my love for her, and her love for me, I was appalled beneath my curiosity and I remembered that to sleep in the light of the full moon is to incubate madness in oneself. Also her head was bigger than a human being's must ever be and her dimples were like craters.

I knew that she was regarding me benignly, but there was terror in the sagacity of her gaze, terror for me, not for her and not for us, just for me and I didn't know why and still don't know. Then it began to ascend, that face, and as it did so it contracted and grew less waxy in form, less pink in colour, acquired hardness, turned almost painfully white as it started to cross the ceiling above me, and I remained on my back and watched and suddenly there were stars around her and these were also faces but faces of other women, not of Hilola, and she outshone them all and I waited for her lips to fall on mine but they never did.

Slowly her head began its descent towards the head of the bed and my own head, and it greatly expanded as it did so, flushed and became amber and wise again, and I felt the chill of an indoor dawn on my skin through the thin blankets, and I dared not ask myself what point she was making with this incredible performance, this lunacy.

Tameris

UNCONDITIONAL LOVE is conditional too. It is conditional on there being no conditions. That's the condition it has. As for my own condition, it was one of relentless curiosity, an infatuation with the repetitive act of patting her hair, her big wiry hair, each strand a tight helix like a spring. I adored touching the hair of sweet Tameris.

Yes, she was sweet, but honey can be dangerous to harvest. Tameris finally rebelled against my obsession, her Circassian eyes flashed with a mischievous fire, the kind that burns the best pages of a book and leaves the boring parts. She was bored with me, evidently, and no longer cared to endure my patting of her vast hair.

It happened this way. I patted it affectionately but with determination as I usually do, my fascination inextricably bound up with my admiration and bafflement, and when I had finished she curled her fingers into a fist and rapped on my forehead as if it was a door. She knocked once, twice, thrice, then stood back a little to wait.

I was astonished to hear grumbling noises from inside my skull and a shuffling sound, as if feet in slippers were reluctantly tramping down an overlong hallway. Tameris smiled ironically. There was no need for her to knock again. The unseen occupant of my head fumbled with bolts and turned an inner handle and suddenly...

My face swung open on hinges and I knew that my soul was standing there quizzically, looking up at the one who had disturbed its repose, and it demanded, "Yes? What do you want?" To which Tameris smiled one of those smiles that are so sweet that anyone who receives one is compelled to brush their teeth afterwards and said:

"I have come to pick you up and take you away."

My soul considered this offer and to my astonishment it agreed to go with her. She reached into my face and plucked it out and together they left the house. With my features in their present condition I was unable to follow. I had to shut my visage securely first, because otherwise anything might happen. A bird might fly into it and get entangled in my thoughts. By the time I was ready it was too late.

Hair today, gone tomorrow. That's a lame joke. My face has lost its resident and like all abandoned properties has started to fall into a state of disrepair. The same way that slates come off a roof, my ideas slide away. And the rafters of my mind are rotting. Tameris, you were my favourite season. With you it was always springtime.

Georgina

NEW YORK IS FAMOUSLY the city that never sleeps, so why are there shops selling beds and bedding there? I have seen them with my own reliable eyes. I asked Georgina to explain the anomaly and she said, "There's no difficulty. Those beds and bedding are not for the local people, who never sleep, but only for export. They are exported to an island on the opposite side of the globe."

"To the antipodes of New York, you mean?" I replied.

"Of course. It's a place where the inhabitants are permanently asleep, to make up for the fact that New Yorkers are always awake, because nature requires balance and there must be a matching debit for every credit. It's a small island but it doesn't need roads or many facilities because nobody ever walks around or engages in any activity other than sleeping. Do you doubt me?"

No, I didn't doubt her, not Georgina, but I wanted more details.

"What is the name of the island?"

"It is the opposite of New York, surely that's obvious?"

"Kroy Wen?" I ventured.

She shook her head. "I said opposite, not backwards. The opposite of New is Old and the opposite of York is... well, York almost sounds like Fork and the opposite of a fork is a spoon, so the answer is that the opposite of York is Upoon. That is the name of the island. *Old Upoon*. It's an odd place."

"How does one get there?"

She shrugged. "Not by any conventional transportation. There is no airport and no ship ever docks at the harbour. The island is surrounded by reefs and the monsters in the dreams of the inhabitants frequently come out of their heads and go for a swim in the waters, so it is a very dangerous place."

"But how do you export the beds and bedding there?"

"We haven't yet managed to find a way," said Georgina sadly, "which is why they are still here and the shops you saw are full of unsold merchandise. Old Upoon is fated never to enjoy the comforts of our commodities and the people will have to remain on hammocks for the foreseeable future."

Siranush (1)

WE WERE TRAVELLING ON the bus and the buildings of the city were flowing past the windows and it occurred to me that maybe the whole thing was a trick and that the bus was standing still and the scenery was on conveyor belts and it was the belts that were moving, not us, and the more I thought about this, the more likely it seemed.

I wanted to test my hypothesis and I shouted to the driver to go faster and because Siranush and myself were the only passengers on board and because it was early morning and because of the urgency in my voice and because he was still slightly drunk from the night before, he obeyed with enthusiasm and pressed on the pedal.

We accelerated or rather I should say that suddenly the conveyor belts outside speeded up. The pedals of the vehicle were obviously connected to the machinery that powered the belts. The buildings slipped past faster and faster, started to blur into each other, but I still shouted for him to go faster and faster. It was the only way.

I was hoping it might be possible to break the conveyor belts and thus expose the illusion. We approached a hill on the outskirts of the city and the downward slope helped to increase our velocity still more. Now there were no buildings but only mountains. We had left the city. At least that's what the designers wanted us to believe.

"Faster!" I cried until the blur outside was a scream. I smelled smoke and knew that the conveyor belts were overheating. Just a little more! The driver was yelling with insane joy. There was an appalling shriek of metal and all at once the scenery outside stopped moving. I had won! The belts had broken down. My victory was total.

And quite unexpectedly, and with great force, Siranush was unable to restrain herself and she flung herself into my arms and we tumbled on the floor and rolled in passionate celebration.

Parisa

"IT'S OUR FIFTH ANNIVERSARY," I said to Parisa that morning, "and not once in our relationship have we argued."

"This is indeed impressive," she replied.

"It is highly unusual. All our friends have argued with their partners at some point. But we are different."

"Not once," she said.

"I wonder why that should be?"

Parisa considered the matter carefully. "Who knows?"

"Because we are so well-suited?"

"No, I don't think that's it. Well-suited couples often argue a lot. Not all argument is unhealthy. It can be good to argue. In fact, never arguing might be said to be quite unnatural."

"I don't feel our relationship is unnatural."

"People argue when they want to convince someone else of their point of view. This means that they care to share their ideas on a subject. But if they don't care what the other person thinks, they are far less likely to try to put their point across. Not arguing could be a sign of apathy, boredom, indifference, or even a lack of love."

"Nonsense! It is a positive value, not a negative."

"I'm only making suggestions."

"Imbecilic suggestions! Why did I even mention it? You clearly can't be trusted to hold a rational debate!"

"You asked me to venture my opinion on why we've never argued. If you can't handle hearing the various options, then you shouldn't have put the question to me in the first place."

"How dare you! The real reason we have never argued is because you are too obstinate and pompous to bother arguing with! Why should I use up my precious time arguing with—"

"Obstinate and pompous? That's rich coming from you, a man who is so full of himself that he always—"

"Full of myself? You are the one who—"

"Liar! You are the most—"

"Why did I ever marry you? What a—"

"Incompetent bastard!"

"Expert bitch!"

And that's how the cataclysmic argument began.

Siranush (2)

WE WERE TRAVELLING ON the bus and heading back towards the city and now I believed it was the bus that was moving and the scenery that stood still. It could be said that I had learned a lesson. As we approached the suburbs of Yerevan I observed that the gaps between the buildings that we passed were getting smaller and smaller. Yes.

What did it mean? I thought about it and the answer soon came to me. It meant that the bus was speeding up. What other explanation could there be? At first a building would pass outside my window and then a minute or more would elapse before another building came along, but that wasn't the way it was happening now. Oh no.

The buildings were passing my window at an increasing rate. Just one a minute became one every ten seconds and then one every two seconds. I was anxious and shouted at the driver to slow down. Because Siranush and myself were the only passengers and because it was late afternoon and because of the urgency in my voice and because he was still slightly dazed from the crash, he replied rudely:

"I am driving at a constant speed, neither faster nor slower. The best thing you can do is shut your mouth."

I didn't know what to say to that but I turned to Siranush for comfort but I made no attempt to embrace her. "You are really a petite woman. I never noticed that before. I don't want to hug you in case I do you some form of injury. You are indeed small."

Those were my words and they astonished me as they came out. She had previously seemed a muscular woman to me, only slightly shorter than myself, but now I saw that in reality she was only the same height as my thumb. Why hadn't I noticed?

Then she spoke but because she was so small it was difficult for me to hear her voice. Yet I think she said:

"I haven't changed my dimensions and I am just as tall as before. But I didn't come back to the city with you. I never boarded the second bus. It seemed safer for me to stay where I was and to make a new life out here in the country, far away from you. The truth is that I'm not smaller, I am just further away. Farewell my dear."

144

Chlöe

I'M VERY RARELY DRUNK and I tend to regard wine as grapes gone wrong but I allowed Chlöe to have her way with me. I was too fond of her perhaps. She poured glasses of a sweet liquid down my throat and I licked my lips and laughed and she drank herself into incoherence too. It was at the end of summer and oranges glowed in the trees at twilight like lanterns with a bird perched here and there as attendants in case they went out. Back to the hotel we staggered up the dim road.

The owner of the taberna waved after us and called out some pleasant remarks that made no real sense and we shouted back some equally inane compliments and slurred a final farewell. Then we were farcically trying to help each other walk with our arms around each other like thick vines and our progress like a stately dance to music with a complex rhythm, an utterly serious matter that was mirthful.

In our room we collapsed onto the bed and giggled at our perfect lack of coordination. I thought for a moment that we were still in the taberna and I called for more retsina but Chlöe lifted her finger to hush me and I strained to understand her words. "Music! We need music!" she said and she nodded at the old gramophone in the corner. I attempted to rise but it was useless. The room began spinning...

The gramophone was out of reach. We were stuck on the bed while a domestic whirlpool rotated the walls around us. I felt seasick and now my giggles turned into sobs, but Chlöe lifted her silencing finger again and I controlled myself with a monumental effort. Music would take our minds off our illness, our drunkenness. How would she manage to climb off the bed and cross the floor to the corner? "Close one eye," she told me, and I did just that, while she did too. And then.

She extended her arm with the hand with the potent finger on the end of it and she lowered it onto the record that had been left on the turntable of the gramophone for who knows how many years. Closing one eye had destroyed parallax and perspective. It looked as if her long and very sharp fingernail rested in the groove of the record.

The room was still spinning for us both. Suddenly there was music, a buzzing of baglamades and bouzoukia, her fingernail playing the part of a stylus as the room revolved at the correct speed. Rebetiko music and now the voice of Roza Eskenazi that entered our ears like extra retsina and no longer did I feel sick but sad instead and yet it was a sadness without any desire for it to go away, a cleansing sadness.

Wines are grapes gone wrong, yes, but Chlöe is a woman who plays music of great intricacy with just one finger.

Ernestina

I WAS TOLD THAT Ernestina was a bodybuilder long before I met her. At that time I was lifting weights myself, expanding the muscles of various parts of my frame, making them denser, delighting in the feeling of power and control this gave me. I was intrigued by the stories I heard about a woman who was building a perfect body on a beach and I decided to visit her and introduce myself and offer my praise.

The journey wasn't a long one in terms of distance so I decided that a bicycle was the only acceptable transportation. My thighs would certainly enjoy the exercise and while I pedalled I thought about Ernestina's thighs and other parts of her. What would she be like in the flesh? Body sculpted to faultlessness on the beach, I pictured her muscle groups oiled by sweat and polished to a gleam by the sunlight.

The roads became narrower, branched into a cluster of lanes, I cruised downhill towards the sea without needing to pedal now. The hedges were impenetrable on both sides and blocked my view. But I smelled the odour of the sea, the ozone and brine and weed and the knees of crabs, dead and alive, and I thought I heard the sliding of shells being rearranged by fussy waves and I knew I was near, very near.

And then I turned a corner and I saw it. The giant made from sand. An immense woman, taller than a church steeple, a veritable colossus, and I applied the brakes and dismounted and squinted hard, because I was sure that Ernestina must be somewhere close, because clearly there had been a misunderstanding and she was a bodybuilder in a different sense, one that builds bodies from scratch, from materials others than flesh, from billions of grains of sand. That she was an artist rather than a fitness fanatic, but I couldn't see anyone at all. The beach was deserted. And I prepared to do two things, to sigh and pedal back home.

Then the giant moved, bent down and scooped up a fistful of wet sand and slapped it on her upper body, on her chest, adding a little more mass to the pectoral muscles there, and I understood that my initial assumption had been right all along and that Ernestina was indeed concerned with the natural process of building her own body.

Anonymia

THERE ARE PLAQUES ON the houses of famous dead people who lived there in former times and these plaques are generally blue. I never questioned her about the implication of her name but I did ask her to take me on a tour of the city and show me all the plaques.

We drank in our fill of past achievements, fixing visionaries to spatial coordinates, and then she said, "There ought to be plaques on the houses of the neighbours of these famous people too, because the neighbour of a famous person is also a little famous."

"But does fame radiate out from its source?"

"Yes, just like heat. The neighbours of the famous person will attract attention by virtue of being in the right place. 'Look, there is so-and-so who lives next door to such-and-such!' This by itself is sufficient. Who wouldn't brag of being a neighbour of someone renowned! There should be plaques on the neighbours' houses."

"But what about the neighbours of the neighbours? Living next door to people who live next door to the famous individual, they have a little fame too. They also should have plaques, of a slightly less vibrant blue. And the process can continue with their neighbours, and so on, the blue growing paler in proportion to its distance from the focus, the wellspring from which the fame burns and flows."

"But the blue will have to start becoming brighter again as the series of plaques eventually approaches the house of another famous individual. It will be like a sine wave travelling between peaks of fame and the palest of the blues will be in the exact centre."

"That's true. And at that centre point will dwell the least famous of all the people on the entire route. Somewhere in this city there's a street with the longest stretch between peaks of fame, and in the middle of this span there is a house in which live the least famous inhabitants of the capital. Who are they? We are unlikely to find out, for the simple reason that they *are* obscure. The fame that's won from being the most unknown example of a thing is hardly the prominent kind."

"But I do know who," she insisted, as she tugged at my elbow to stop me in my tracks. We were walking along the pavement of an extremely long street. I turned to look at the house we were standing outside. There was a plaque on the wall and it was such a pale blue it was almost white. There were no words on it. It was blank. Anonymia had a key in her hand and she added, "It's our house. Let's go inside and make ourselves at home."

Monica

A doughnut without holes
    is a Danish
and so are you.
I doughnut see any holes
    out of place
       on your face.

You are not a flute
or a motorway underpass.
    But I bet Bang
      & Olufsen
      designed you
        at least in part.

Alice

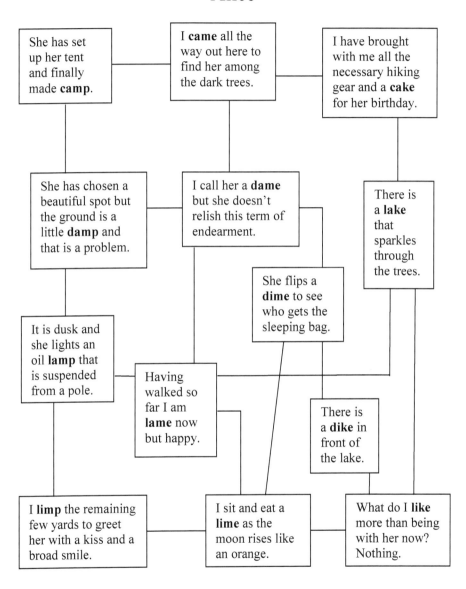

She has set up her tent and finally made **camp**.

I **came** all the way out here to find her among the dark trees.

I have brought with me all the necessary hiking gear and a **cake** for her birthday.

She has chosen a beautiful spot but the ground is a little **damp** and that is a problem.

I call her a **dame** but she doesn't relish this term of endearment.

There is a **lake** that sparkles through the trees.

She flips a **dime** to see who gets the sleeping bag.

It is dusk and she lights an oil **lamp** that is suspended from a pole.

Having walked so far I am **lame** now but happy.

There is a **dike** in front of the lake.

I **limp** the remaining few yards to greet her with a kiss and a broad smile.

I sit and eat a **lime** as the moon rises like an orange.

What do I **like** more than being with her now? Nothing.

Rebekah

IF THE DEAD SEA is really the lowest point on the surface of the Earth, as we are often informed, why don't all bicycles, motor vehicles and balls roll there, and why doesn't all long hair tend to flow in that direction?

Then I realised that actually I *had* ended up on its shores and that I was on roller skates and I'd come a long dusty way, an enormous distance, my thirst was immense too, and the tang on my tongue of salt made it painful for me to lick my lips, but here I was with Rebekah, and she was with me.

Her hair was red and when I reached out to stroke it, the pain of fire leapt up my fingers and I pulled away. I touched her ear instead, twisted it gently, playfully, and I was astonished to see her hair change colour. Now it was blue. I took her other ear in my other hand and twisted that one as well.

The hair changed back to red. I understood that her hair was like water, the water a thirsty man craved so badly, and that her ears were like taps. This amused me even though I was aware it shouldn't have done.

I played with her ears, turning first one, then the other. The red was always too hot and the blue always too cold, but eventually I managed to obtain a perfect mix, a light flow that was a lukewarm purple, and then I washed my hands in it, humming as I did so, while Rebekah observed me in silence.

I planned to finish washing and then to turn one of her ears off completely and the other to maximum to obtain a cold gush that I could use to slake my thirst, but before I had the chance to do this, Rebekah reached out and took hold of my nose and with a snarl of fury she twisted it and kept twisting.

My own hair didn't change colour or temperature, not even slightly. But there was water and it did pour out of me. It erupted from my eyes. Then Rebekah kicked me and started me rolling towards the sea and I couldn't stop myself, I was unable to see clearly, and I trundled into the shallows and floated there like a bicycle, car or ball, all misshapen, and soon the salt of my tears merged with the salt of that lake that is both a fable and a truth, a parable and a reward.

Samantha

IN THE CANADIAN WILDERNESS, far from the nearest settlement, among the mountains, the forests, the lakes, and we knew there were bears, many bears, dangerous bears, bears that hug you not to express affection but to crush your internal organs into mush, and we wore little bells to warn them we were coming. But as we tinkled over fallen trees and across the stepping-stones of a stream, she asked me something that had bothered her since we set off before the quiet

153

dawn.

"Surely the bells alert the bears to our presence and will attract them? I don't see how wearing them makes us any safer. We're advertising our presence. We are telling them that food is on its way just like a dinner bell. We are like a perverse main course during a banquet that calls its own diners."

I shrugged. "We were advised to wear bells and that's all I know. It could be that bears don't really want to meet any human beings out here in the great outdoors. We might be minor annoyances to them rather than walking snacks. I don't know. Your logic sounds good but it is rather alarming."

We passed up a slope into a region of dense black spruce trees. The silence might have been ominous, but how could we know? Our bells tinkled mournfully and any silence existing there prior to our arrival had fled. But in fact we weren't alone, dark shapes moved through the trees, bulky forms converged. We were being watched and the pressure of this scrutiny was tangible. Our boots slipped in the mud as if we were being physically pushed back down the slope.

Bears? I already felt their hot breath on my face but only in my imagination. And then Samantha said, "They are bells. We have summoned bells. We are wearing the young and these are the adults. Big bells…"

And so they were. Church bells. Vast and

154

brassy, the feral descendants of ancient bells that had escaped from belfries and steeples long ago, perhaps centuries ago, and migrated here, away from the cities and the bell-ringers who tormented them, away to the wilds, to the pristine corners of the world.

They began ringing, booming, thundering, clappers like clenched fists on the ends of sweeping arms, the arms of trapped goblins hammering desperately to get out of their campaniform prisons, goblins that were very ursine in appearance, goblins that might actually have been bears, angry bears...

"What should we do?" I cried.

Samantha recalled her upbringing, her early devotion.

"They are performing for us. Full-circle ringing. This is a complex ritual and because there are eight of those monster bells they have the option of giving us a set of changes called tittums. This is going to take a long time. It might strike you as quite discordant, so just grin and bear it."

"Strike me... bear it..." I heeded only the puns in her answer.

And then we were enveloped.

I still don't know if those bells were living beings or whether they really did have goblins or bears inside them. I looked inside one of the little bells I was wearing later but saw no creatures of any sort. We remained until the end of the performance out of politeness and because to run

155

away might have been a *casus belli* for them, a fine reason to go to war with these two intruders. When they fell silent, we pushed on past them, tinkling as we went, like kidnappers or lepers.

Verniana

WE WERE FEELING BLUE, as many of us often do. I was in a funk as dense as fog and she was too. Truly I was blue.

And yet good things come out of the blue, this is something we know, but who stops to wonder where that mysterious blue is located? Verniana and I agreed to look for it but we already knew in our heart of hearts that we were dwelling within it. We merely had to activate it, to make it pulse like that deep heart inside those hearts. If we voyaged into the blue distance we would leave the blues behind and eventually return to the better blue.

There was only one way. I was in a funk like a fog, so let me be Fogg, and she was the one with a nose for a clue, so let her be Passepartout. The solution was adventurous and fictive. "We'll be like characters in a story, but I have felt that way for a long time."

"Because we already *are* characters in a story."

"In this book, the volume being read right now, yes. But I don't mean that. I mean that we will be just like—"

"Jules Verne heroes."

Oh yes! We would travel the entire planet together and finally return to our starting point and this circumnavigation must be completed in how many days or ways? "Around the world in eighty lays—" I began but her abrupt fury cut dead the words in my mouth. "That's the plan, selfish and nefarious rascal that you are?" she cried.

"But no!" I protested and tried in vain to explain.

Because that is the way simple misunderstandings grow bigger, break out of their confines, rampage through emotions and histories, and thus I had to endure her chastisement before I stood a chance of demonstrating why it was unnecessary, why I was pure.

"The man who aspires to sleep his way around the world? That's what this book has been about from the beginning? An atavistic and libidinous catalogue of self-indulgent memoir mixed with daydreams? A priapic list of beddable lovelies masquerading as a celebration of feminine diversity? Eighty women from eighty different countries and cultures, but you as the focal point? How transparent your motives suddenly are! How bogus and deceitful your lyricism and inventions!"

"But I didn't finish my sentence," I pleaded.
"Do so now," she said.
"Around the world in eighty lazy days…"

"Not lays, eh? Lazy?"

It made sense. And it was the truth. No need to rush. The days didn't need to be consecutive, they didn't need to follow one after another, they could come whenever they chose. Lazy days, yes, but not sleepy ones. It was time to set off. Steam train, balloon, elephant. Who knew? But slow, always slow, grandly slow, like the blue sky lapping the horizon on clear days, like continental drift, like colliding galaxies, the knitting of jellyfish bones, the ticking of fossilised clocks, the accidental solving of a logical paradox, the decay of irrational metaphors.

Envoi

ENVOI IS NOT A woman, but a few concluding words. *World Muses* is not a work about a man with eighty different girlfriends, but one that consists of eighty different routines about one man and one woman. The situations are not sequential in time or space. They are only what-ifs? It is a garden of forking paths, or perhaps a nested box of universes. Nor am I the man. Scenes that are autobiographical, or that take inspiration from real life and people, are vastly outnumbered by those that are pure invention. The force that drives the events in these parallel fictions is not libido but respect for diversity.

This is an important distinction to make in a society that has grown distrustful of infatuation.

The few experimental pieces among the escapades and rodomontades are self-explanatory only in Utopia. The tale called 'Söökhlö' is one of a set of grid stories that owe their creation to the existence of OuLiPo, that wondrous French workshop in which arbitrary mathematical and logical constraints are invented and applied to texts. The constraint in this case is one I call $\geq 2n+1$ (greater or equal to 2n plus one) and it creates grids that can be read across every row and down every column and along the main diagonals. Those are the deliberate microfictions but accidental ones may exist on other diagonals, in reverse directions on columns and rows and in non-linear ramblings throughout the grids.

The tale called 'Alice' is based on word ladders, that delightful puzzle invented by Lewis Carroll in which a word changes one letter in order to transform into another (coherent) word, the process continuing for as long as possible. The transformational words are highlighted in the text itself and the paragraphs are linked according to whether they are the next step in the ladder or not. The result is a story formed of pseudo-non-sequiturs. This word ladder is more like scaffolding, for it diverges at several points and spreads sideways as well as elongating itself vertically. The frame is the point of the story and thus frames itself.

W   M

   O   U

       R   H   Y   S

   L   E

D   S

      H   U   G   H   E   S

Author's Note

For this paperback edition, five bonus fictions have been added. The rigours of typesetting are responsible for that. White space appeared beneath some of the chapters due to the more experimental pieces requiring a full page in isolation. An opportunity arose to include extra material and I took it. These bonus fictions are 'Arabella', 'Lowri', 'Esther', 'Jane' and 'Monica'. In fact, the chapter called 'Emily' here is called 'Esther' in the hardback edition, but it was impossible to change the name of the new Esther, as *her* chapter relies entirely on wordplay concerned with her name. The old Esther could undergo a name change with no harmful effects whatsoever. The order of some of the pieces is slightly different too, again for reasons of typesetting. Form makes a difference to content and that's the way it should be. The fact there are now eighty-five muses instead of just eighty means that the protagonists of 'Verniana' are in even more of a muddle than before, but that's life and literature for you. And yes, this book is for you and only you, and it will forever remain truly, secretly, whimsically yours.

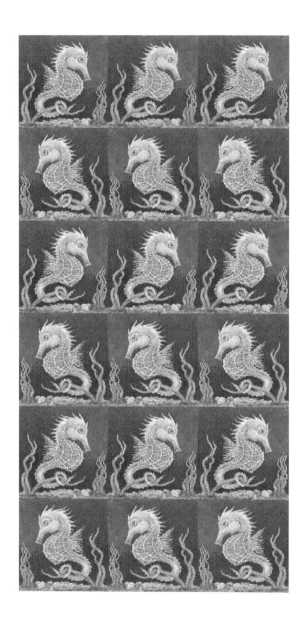

162

W						M
	O				U	
		R	H	Y	S	
			L	E		
			S	D		
	H	U	G	H	E	S

Made in the USA
Middletown, DE
13 January 2018